Shadowed

&

Sentimental

BY

Ine

Contents

Contents cont.

Blueberry Pie

With bare hands, Clair mixed together flour, sugar and butter. Then she added egg and milk, the way Granny Kirkpatrick had taught her. She smiled, remembering licking her fingers when Granny wasn't looking.

Now, her fingers sensed the dough was the right consistency. Wrapping it in a tea towel, she placed it in the fridge to rest. She took another wrapped lump of dough from the fridge, flattening and shaping it with a wooden rolling pin. She lined two dishes with pastry, filled them with blueberries then made pastry lids. She was confident her pies would be perfect. Granny had taught her well.

Granny Kirkpatrick was special. She had always been there to wipe away tears, give hugs and do all the things grannies were meant to do.

Placing the pies in the oven, Clair was flooded with childhood memories of Granny's kitchen. They had worked together, one teaching and guiding, the other watching, listening and learning. The woman and the young girl had shared a comfortable companionship as they measured, weighed, sifted, kneaded and mixed.

Clair cleaned the kitchen bench in order to prepare the last pies for baking. It was late afternoon and she had been working all day. The aroma of fresh baking permeated the house. Blueberry pies covered the dining room table.

An excellent cook, Granny was renowned for her blueberry pies, baking them for church and school fetes and the CWA. They had even been raffled for the fire brigade. Surveying her own work, Clair knew that Granny had taught her more than the art of cooking. One becoming grey and frail, the other strong and robust, through the years, they shared secrets and told stories. From these special times, Clair had gained much wisdom for life's journey.

The last pies were placed on cooling racks. Clair's work for today was nearly done. Several hundred people were expected to attend tomorrow's funeral. Granny Kirkpatrick would approve of blueberry pie with dollops of cream served at her wake in the church hall.

Where Are You?

At the break of day
I look for you sleeping innocently
in the crook of my arm.
I look for you on swings
in noisy play grounds
alongside busy streets
with your small legs kicking excitedly.
I think I once saw you running
through autumn leaves in May.
You had grown taller
and your black hair was longer.
I think I once saw your smile
on another child's face.
I can tell you've been near
when I catch an echo of your voice.
Child of my womb, where are you now?

A Hum From The Past

A fine drizzle was falling as Dorothy paused and looked at the old house. It was a familiar sight, she passed it every time she went to the shops but she'd always had a strange sort of affinity with old empty houses. She felt that, if you cared to listen, they were full of voices telling stories from the past.

Gazing at the overgrown garden, Dorothy decided she would help herself to some of the port wine magnolia flowers on her way home. Perhaps it was stealing but they were just going to waste. She'd take some of the pink camellias as well. They would look nice on the side table in the sitting room. She unconsciously rubbed her bare ring finger as she continued to the shops.

"What will it be today, Dorothy?"

The butcher knew her well. Still thinking about the old house, it took her a moment to reply. She bought lamb chops and sausages then went to the bakery.

The house had been there as long she could remember. She'd grown up and lived with her parents just around the corner until she married Claude and moved away. They moved back into her parents' house after her mother died. They had been there ever since.

Dorothy bought bread rolls and apricot slices at the bakery, apples and avocados at the green grocers then stamps from the post office. Some of Claude's friends were coming to play cards in the afternoon so she ought to be getting home.

Long wet grass brushed her legs as she picked the

magnolia and camellia blossoms and carefully placed them in her shopping bag. This garden was beautiful when she was a child. There used to be fruit trees and a vegetable garden out the back. *The house has changed hands many times; I wonder what's there now. I'll have a quick peek.*

She walked past a wall with high windows, added many years ago. She resisted the urge to look through a hole in the door of the big garage and turned the corner into the back yard. It was unrecognisable, littered with decrepit sheds and bungalows, concrete slabs, blackberry vines and neglected garden beds.

Looking towards the house she saw that part of the back wall was missing where renovations had been started then stopped. Some of the interior walls and floorboards were also missing. It was like gaping wounds and Dorothy wondered if she should avert her eyes. If only she could mend it, make it complete and protect it from the prying eyes of others. She wanted most of all to protect the stories from the past. To protect them from spilling out and somehow being lost without anyone having heard them. Rubbing her ring finger, she walked away with a peculiar ache in her heart.

Dorothy told Claude about the house and its abandoned renovations. "I wonder who owns it now." He was more interested in eating lunch. She didn't tell him how uneasy she felt.

Her ring finger was rubbed more than usual that afternoon. She'd developed the habit after her wedding ring disappeared many years ago. She did it more often when she was upset or anxious. What happened to her ring was a mysterious tragedy she had never gotten over.

Her wedding ring was a beautiful thing. A gold band inset with three tiny rubies. She and Claude chose it together. Their entwined initials were engraved on the inside. She had no engagement ring because Claude couldn't afford one at the time. Dorothy said that the wedding ring was more than sufficient. Now it was gone forever.

They had been painting the kitchen. Dorothy hadn't wanted her precious ring to be spoiled so she removed it and placed it on the dressing table. It was gone when she looked for it later. They both searched the house over and over but never found it. Someone must have come through the open bedroom window and stolen it. Dorothy still shuddered whenever she thought about it. There had been other thefts in the neighbourhood, portable radios, garden tools, push bikes and the like. People speculated about the identity of the thief and there was talk about it being someone who lived in the old house.

Dorothy never got another ring. Nothing could replace the original.

She felt compelled to look at the old house again. It was as though it was calling her, telling her to hurry. Claude said she would probably be trespassing so she waited till Monday when he went to bowls. She hurried down the street as soon as he left.

There was a sign saying the owner planned to build home units at the back. If she wanted to look inside, she would have to do it before the builders came.

She wondered if anyone was watching as she slipped between the timber frames that once supported the back wall. Interior walls were also missing. The house was just a shell, but it wasn't empty. Echoes of past inhabitants remained. The sound of a young boy's laughter came from the front of the house. Carefully making her way across the timber floor, she knew it was Cedric. Memories of playing hide and seek with the freckled faced boy came flooding back. She smelt the aroma of hot Milo and freshly baked biscuits and heard Cedric's mother calling from the kitchen. She wondered where they were now and wished their families had stayed in touch.

Dorothy reached an open fire place in what used to be the lounge room. The blackened grate was broken. The once elegant marble mantelpiece was cracked and, in places, no longer attached to the brick wall. She touched the hard, cold marble and listened.

The air vibrated with the hum of voices, laughter and sometimes weeping. The house was offering up its stories to her. Stories of love and hope, sorrow and despair, triumphs and disasters. The stories of all the people who once lived here were humming in the timber, the bricks, the roof and the window panes. Dorothy tried to separate the sounds one from the other. She wanted to hear every single story.

Something shining in a crack between the marble mantle piece and the brick wall caught her eye. It looked like a gold ring. She heard only the beating of her heart. She took a nail file from her handbag and carefully slid it down behind the shiny object then slowly pushed it upwards. Eventually, she plucked it up between two fingers and stared at it. The three little rubies were still there and so were the entwined initials.

The old house remained quiet and still. Perhaps she had heard the only story she needed to hear. Her knuckles were too knobbly now for the ring to fit her finger. She would need to have it enlarged.

The Forest Of Memories

Raised up on its front legs, the lizard was motionless except for the flickering of its eyes. Suddenly, it darted through the fallen leaves and wiry grass. Its thin body making barely a sound; just a suggestion of a rustle. It stopped close against the trunk of a eucalypt, blending in with the sap stains on the peeling bark. Almost imperceptibly, a thick tongue, the colour of ink, darted from its pointed head and scooped up a passing ant. Watchful eyes surveyed the territory again before it darted off to another spot.

Adjusting his backpack, Jason watched the lizard until it vanished into thick undergrowth. His lean, fit physique could be attributed to years of trekking and mountain climbing in South Africa. The forest, its lizards and other creatures were part of the bitter sweet memories that lay nestled in his soul. Sometimes they lay hidden from his awareness. Sometimes they taunted him with the sensation of tasting velvet smooth chocolate and then finding it gone before he had fully savoured it, leaving his tongue hungering for more.

Twenty years is a long time, he thought, *what if the track no longer exists? But I've found the forest so I can find the spot.*

He was deeper in the forest now, surrounded by tall, straight eucalyptus trees, some with massive trunks. The humid air was thick with their smell mixed with mustiness rising from the forest floor. A breeze rustled the tops of the trees far above him. Twigs and small branches descended to the ground with sharp cracking noises. Leaves floated earthward with barely a whisper. Jason surveyed his surroundings. *I hope this place is never logged.*

A green parrot, startled by Jason's presence, took wing, screeching through the tree tops. Molly had known the names of most of the birds in the forest. *"Shush1 don't move. Don't make a sound,"* she had said, her dark eyes shining with happiness as she stood gazing at a parrot or a honey eater. Her long hair fell down her back like a river of rippling black silk.

These days, his own brown hair was greying around the temples. He kept it cropped short. That way, it was easier to wear a hard hat. *Nothing stays the same, except for the emptiness inside.*

Earlier in the day, he had stopped his car on the verge of a hill and looked back towards Brisbane. The city had changed in his absence. Glass and concrete edifices stood where factories and timber houses had been; apartment buildings lined the banks of the river where park land or scrub had existed. The city and suburbia had expanded, but he had managed to find the essence of the city he had once known.

Returning to the suburbs, the streets, the places of his childhood, he had found things that were unchanged except for the natural process of passing years. Timber houses on high stumps, painted with the new weather resistant paint; ancient jacaranda and Moreton bay fig trees and cemeteries holding history in their graves. He had found gardens and parks filled with old fashioned roses, the kind that had strong sweet perfume and long treacherous thorns. Yes! The essence of the city hadn't changed.

The essence of the man hadn't changed either. His body had grown harder, leaner and he had learned new things, changed some of his ideas, made mistakes, stumbled and fallen, only to get up go on. The centre of his being had remained unchanged. Jason had known this all along but was only just beginning to accept it, to stop fighting it. He was still in love with Molly.

Brushing aside a thorny vine, he found the path. It was not overgrown and lost, as he had feared, but well worn. He stood for a moment, taking in the sounds of the forest. High above him, the raucous laugh of a kookaburra echoed through the forest. It was answered by another, then another, then yet more until it seemed the entire world was filled with their harsh, grating laughter. For a moment, it was like nothing else existed. Just the sound of the kookaburras. Grinning to himself, he asked, *Do you think that I'm a fool or are you happy that I've found the path?* The noise died down but for several minutes the birds took turns at chuckling loudly to each other across the forest roof. *One of you bastards probably just feasted on a brown lizard!* He thought but he held no rancour, *That's nature!*

He walked slowly now. There was something comforting about being alone in the warm dappled light of the forest. Pausing, he touched the white trunk of a eucalypt with his hand. Through the eyes of an engineer, he saw beauty in its strength and height. His large, long fingered hands felt its hardness and the irregularities in its smoothness. In places hidden from sunlight, Molly's body had been pale and smooth. There were no irregularities. Just smoothness.

"The trees are magnificent, aren't they?" Jason's hands were still stroking the tree as the middle aged couple stopped to talk.

"I love them." He resented the intrusion but there was no point in being rude.

The man, resting one foot on a log, seemed ready for a long chat. "We came across a goanna on the side of the track just a little further along."

"Oh. I will keep a watch out for it. I hope it's still there." Jason spoke with a clipped accent.

The woman asked, "Where are you from? That doesn't sound like an Aussie accent."

He hadn't felt like chatting, but their eager friendliness was a welcome contrast to the aloofness of many people in Johannesburg. He told them he had been born in Brisbane and how, twenty years ago, at the age of nineteen, he had gone to South Africa with his parents and younger brother. They were keen to hear all about South Africa so it was some time before Jason said "I'd better be going."

He came across the goanna stretched out on a log. Like the brown lizard, its eyes continuously monitored its surroundings while it lay perfectly still. The tongue flicking in and out of its mouth was long and thin.

A little further along, there were was a wooden picnic table and benches in the middle of a clearing. This was new since he had walked here with Molly. They had eaten apples and shared a bottle of warm lemonade whilst they sat leaning against the trunk of a tree.

Now he poured hot, milky coffee into the top of his thermos flask and sat on one of the benches. A magpie watched him from a short distance, and then grew braver and perched on a far corner of the table. As it edged its black and white feathers closer to him, its lighter coloured, slightly smaller female companion joined it. Staring at Jason, they both began a melodic, high pitched warble. *Sly buggers,* Jason thought as he broke a health bar in two and threw the pieces in their direction. He didn't know if health bars were good for magpies. Molly had told him that she fed scraps of raw meat them when they visited her back yard.

Finishing his coffee, Jason walked past the edge of the clearing back into the forest. There was no path here, but he instinctively knew the way. He could feel the presence of Molly in the forest and hear her in the breeze that rustled the canopy overhead. Her smell mingled with the perfume of eucalypt and mustiness.

"I will come back for you," he had said. *When I came back, Molly, you had vanished.*

Her father had roared at him in a thick Irish brogue, "I have no daughter and I don't talk to heathens like you!" He had slammed the door in Jason's face.

As tears spilled from hr eyes, the old woman next door had spoken in broken English. "I don't know where she go love. She a beautiful girl, love, beautiful. She said she go far away to have the baby. I no hear from her anymore." Bereft, he had gone back to Johannesburg and tried to forget.

***

The ancient tree in front of him had withstood the elements. Fire had hollowed out the bottom of its trunk leaving an arch shaped gap. *Look! We could walk through that!* Molly has said. He had needed to crouch, but Molly had managed to scrape through without crouching. She emerged triumphantly and laughed as she fell into his arms. What followed next was inevitable.

Her body was warm and soft, yet strong and firm, moulding against him a he pulled her closer. Her lips yielded to the hunger of his mouth. The litter on the forest floor made a scratchy bed but they barely noticed the twigs denting their flesh. They were both awkward and clumsy. He had been afraid of hurting her but, by the time she cried out, he was intoxicated by his passion and her nearness. He no longer had control. Molly's cry turned to soft moaning as her arms increased their grip and her lips covered his face with frantic kisses.

Now the forest floor echoed with memories that were etched in his brain; memories he once thought he could erase. Jason walked back to the picnic table where he had left the back pack. He had finally stopped fighting the memories. He would not be returning to Johannesburg. He would find the beautiful girl who had gone far away to have his baby.

Broken

I wanted a place to unravel my thoughts in private. I didn't feel capable of social chatter but it was too late to turn and go home. I had promised Wendy I'd visit her after work and she probably witnessed my arrival through her kitchen window. The door opened before I rung the bell.

"Freya! You look exhausted. Come in."

I tried to smile, "It's been a long day."

I waited in the lounge room while Wendy went to the kitchen. Before long, she brought tea and scones, saying something about her son. My mind was so scattered, I barely heard her. Trying to anchor my thoughts, I watched her pour tea from her favourite rose patterned porcelain pot. My eyes were drawn to a fine line around the spout. "What happened to the teapot?"

"I knocked it against the kitchen tap. It was still beautiful even though it was broken so I mended it." She began to explain about the special glue she used but was stopped mid-sentence by my sobbing.

During my long years as an Emergency Department Nurse, I had learned to lock my emotions away so that I could work without hindrance. I never learned how to keep them locked away. Invariably, as I changed out of uniform, they would break free. Sometimes, they hit me with such ferocity; I wondered how much longer I could go on.

Now my mind was filled with the vision of a bloodied, bruised, young man. Barely twenty, his tanned athletic body lay unmoving on a trolley. Blood matted his short brown hair. A gash across his forehead looked obscene on such youthful flesh. His upper torso was bruised purple where his ribs had been crushed against a steering wheel. He was still beautiful, even though he was broken, but, unlike Wendy's teapot, we were unable to mend him.

I doubt if anyone could fully understand the extent of my anguish but I was thankful for a good friend as Wendy put her arms around me.

The Landscape of My Mind

I wandered upon a dark valley in the landscape of my mind, a place full of muted sighs and weeping. Breezes in tree tops whispered of deception and broken promises. A shallow, sluggish creek murmured about war and destruction, poverty and greed. I wept for an insect struggling to escape a spider web in the branches of a spindly bush. I feared that my soul, like the insect, would die so I left that valley of gloom.

I stumbled over a bump in the landscape of my mind. It was just a grassy hillock, a minor detail that caught me unawares. I limped on, my eyes focussed on a lofty peak ahead. Alas! I tripped once, twice, many times. A stone, a rut, a tiny hollow joined forces to impede my way. At last, I saw the wisdom hidden in seemingly insignificant things.

I've climbed mountains in the landscape of my mind. Unbidden, they rose to block my path. Coward that I am, I didn't bravely meet their challenge. I lay in the shadows, dispirited and helpless before crawling from my torpor and scrambling upwards. I lost my footing and tumbled down but started again, groping for new footholds and crevices for my fingers. I climbed higher, only to be dashed by an avalanche. I wailed in despair and wearily tried again. Bruised and battered, I clawed my way to the summit and gazed at the vista before me. My spirit, barely comprehending the lessons from the climb, filled with joy because I was free to take any path I chose.

There's a volcano in the landscape of my mind. It's an unpredictable and untamed beast that gives no warning before erupting with regurgitated anger about eons of injustices. I tremble in its presence and can only gaze on it from afar.

I've crossed a desert in the landscape of my mind. Blinded by harshness, my starved soul became dry and withered. Then, at my lowest ebb, I reached out and was nourished by the strength and courage of the desert plants and creatures.

I've found a comfortable bed among fertile fields and perfumed gardens. I've trod the landscape of my mind and found myself.

 # Drum Beat 

The party was a noisy affair. Against my better judgement, I had gone to please a friend who had once helped me out of a tight fix. I felt indebted to him.

The hot, crowded room was the perfect environment for claustrophobia. Thirty or forty people milled around exchanging gossip and jokes. They shouted to be heard above the African drum beat churning out of a juke box in one corner. Some gyrated to the rhythm. From time to time, a woman wearing a low cut red dress, emitted laughter so shrill it made all the other noise pale into insignificance.

My head pounded to the beat of the drums. I retrieved my coat and handbag from a pile on a divan, sure no one would miss me as I slipped out the door into the night.

The echo of the drums battered my brain as the train carried me through the suburbs. I longed for a warm bath and some aspirin and wished the train would go faster.

I stepped from the train onto a deserted platform. The dark cold night wrapped around me and the drums went on pounding my brain. I was pleased my house was only two streets away.

Suddenly, two figures loomed before me; shadows in the darkness. I felt my handbag being snatched from my grasp as something hard struck me across the forehead.

Now, as I lie on the pavement, there is no sound except that made by footsteps. Footsteps running away. Rubber soled shoes pounding on concrete, the noise fading into the distance.

Those footsteps have gone but I hear others. The footsteps of my mother, firm and sure. They change, becoming slow and shuffling; shuffling through my head. I want to say, "Stop. Wait a while," but no words come from my mouth.

Now there is the sound of heavy work boots. I know it's my father, his footsteps marching through my head and down the long, dark street.

The footsteps increase, walking, marching, running, dancing, all at once. Footsteps of children, old men and women and of athletes sprinting down a running track. The sound crowds my head. Hundreds of footsteps going in every direction, never stopping, never pausing. I must scream, tell them to stop, go away, and cease their torturing of me.

Voices mingle with the footsteps. Someone calls my name. "Are you awake? Can you hear me?" Someone leans over me. Through blurred vision, I focus on the thing hanging around his neck. It is a stethoscope.

A voice says, "Can you squeeze my hand?"

I ask for some aspirin.

The Fiddle and Bow

Meet me around eight
At the Fiddle and Bow
Don't be late
Or you'll miss the show.

It's quite upbeat
Down a little lane
Just off Smith Street
Close to the train.

Meet me around eight
It's now past ten
And far too late
I won't see him again!

I've walked the streets
Seen no Fiddle and Bow
No place all upbeat
I've missed the show.

Meet me around eight
I'm left in the lurch
I thought I had a date
I'm out on a perch.

I've trudged Smith Street
Searched every lane
He's a lying cheat
Just causing me pain.

I'm back to square one
Struck a cruel blow
Fiddled and done
He's broken my bow.

The Stooped Old Man

The boy hugged his scrawny chest as icy wind blew through his thin jacket. His bare feet were numbed with cold; one big toe bleeding where he had stubbed it. He hurried as dark clouds gathered overhead. He could do without a soaking and, besides, he was hungry. He had to buy bread and soup bones so his mother could feed the family that evening.

A stooped old man brushed past and something fell from the pocket of his overcoat. The boy scooped it up. "Sir! Wait! You dropped a coin."

The old man turned and looked at the boy with faded but kind blue eyes. "You may keep it."

The coin was unlike any the boy had seen before. It was metal, but not silver or gold, and engraved with a stooped old man, just like the one standing before him. "But it's yours, Sir. I can't keep it."

"I want you to have it. Keep it with you at all times. You will know when to pass it on." Reaching into another pocket, he produced a pair of shoes. "Try these on."

The shoes were a perfect fit and, not quite believing what was happening, the boy bent to tie the laces. When he looked up, the old man was gone.

***

"Thomas, wherever did you get those shoes?"

The boy told his mother about the stooped old man. "And that's not all. The baker gave me yesterday's bread for free and the butcher sold me meaty sheep shanks for the price of soup bones."

Thomas kept the coin in his pocket. When he slept, he placed it under his pillow. He often thought of the old man and how good fortune had followed him ever since their meeting. His feet, of course, grew too big for the shoes but he soon owned many shoes. His father found good employment and his mother was able to put a hearty meal on the table each evening.

Many years later, Thomas's children loved to hear the story about the stooped old man, though they weren't sure if it was true. They were never allowed to hold the strange coin for more than a brief moment before Thomas tucked it into a pocket.

Thomas told the story to his grandchildren and, in time, to his great grandchildren. Just the other day, a freckled faced lad looked into his faded blue eyes and asked, "Was the stooped old man just like you, Great Grandpa?" Thomas hadn't realized just how bent his back had become.

Later, as was his habit, Thomas took a walk in the nearby park. A damp mist hung in the air but his coat kept him warm. He absently played with the old coin and, suddenly, it fell out of his pocket.

"Hey, Mister, you dropped something."

He turned to see a thin boy wearing no shoes. "You can keep it. You will know when to pass it on."

Scrub Ticks

Lilliana's restaurant cafe exuded old world charm. Delicately patterned fine china plates hung from picture rails around the pale beige walls; an embossed copper screen stood in front of a fireplace and porcelain dolls graced each end of the mantelpiece. During holiday seasons and on weekends, Lilliana's was busy with every table occupied. It was now midweek and just a few diners were enjoying a late lunch, no doubt after a pleasant drive through the Dandenongs. The murmur of voices and occasional laughter could be heard above Tony O'Conner mood music playing in the background.

The grey haired man and woman dining at a table tucked away in a recess might have been part of the decor. Slender figures gave the impression of frailty; yet their faces were handsome and had weathered the years well. They forked dainty portions of quiche and salad into prim mouths, occasionally touching serviettes to their lips. Between mouthfuls, they conversed earnestly, stopping whenever Jill, the waitress passed nearby.

Finishing the last of her quiche and smoothing her cream linen skirt with thin, well-manicured hands, the woman asked "Shall we order coffee, George?" He responded by beckoning a waitress.

Jill had anticipated the coffee order. They were frequent customers with set habits. They always ordered quiche followed by cappuccino. Sometimes they came twice in a month; sometimes several months elapsed between visits. The staff speculated about their identity and why they were so secretive. In the end, it was decided that they were having an illicit affair.

Miranda stirred two spoons of sugar into her coffee, a crease appearing between her carefully shaped, greying eyebrows. "Bendigo is urgent. We should deal with it soon, George."

He adjusted the cuffs of his white shirt. "Let me see... Yes, I will go the day after tomorrow. They won't know I am coming."

"Don't go on your own. You will need to be careful."

"It's urgent but it's really just an irritating itch caused by a scrub tick. Ticks crawl out backwards if you smother them with a bit of Vaseline and I've got just the right kind of Vaseline. I will take Tony with me."

"I'm sure you will know how to deal with it." She took a chocolate from beside her coffee cup and bit off a tiny portion. "Delicious! I wonder where they get them from." Her speech was refined, her voice well-modulated.

"I will ask on the way out. I believe someone's birthday is coming up soon." He pointed a teaspoon in her direction before using it to scoop froth from his cup.

Her laughter sounded above the background music. "You are so thoughtful, George. It's a pleasure to do business with you."

Jill suppressed a giggle as George reached across the table to take Miranda's hand in his, then drew it towards him and kissed it. *How very sweet and romantic,* she thought. *That just proves they are having an affair.*

They exited the restaurant together, leaving behind a subtle smell of perfume and after shave. Jill cleared the table, taking the used crockery and cutlery to the kitchen. "They are such a lovely old couple," she said to Joe, the kitchen hand, "I wonder when they will be back,"

"You're just a romantic! From what you tell me, there's

something really odd about those two."He shook his head as he rinsed dishes.

A fortnight later, Jill was surprised when a younger man accompanied the couple. His dark hair was cut close to his head and a white tee shirt accentuated his lean, muscular torso. He ordered steak and chips which, when he wasn't speaking animatedly, he ate with gusto. From time to time, he gesticulated with his fork, gold rings glinting on several of his fingers.

"I ask you, what kind of fool would refuse to have insurance?" he said just as Jill passed to serve another customer.

"Are you enjoying your steak, Tony?" George changed the subject and, when Jill was out of hearing distance, "You will need to speak more quietly if we are to meet in places like this."

"Yeah. Well they need to learn is all I can say. It just takes one or two like that and soon everyone else follows suit."

"It seems like there might be a major outbreak of scrub ticks if preventive steps aren't taken." Miranda poked at lettuce leaves with a fork. "We need you to come up with an extermination plan, Tony."

"I'm working on it. Of course there might be extra fees involved for such a complicated and delicate matter."

George's face grew tense. "A bonus based on the degree of success would seem reasonable. We can discuss that later. Let's order coffee now."

The younger man seemed odd company for such a refined and gentle couple and, intrigued, Jill passed by their table more often than necessary. She noticed how they lowered their voices whenever she passed. She also noticed they seemed worried about something. When she spoke about it with Joe, he said "I tell you, they are up to no good."

They didn't return for a good month. They seemed changed. Their stride was less confident; there were dark circles around their eyes; her hair looked neglected and his white shirt was creased. They both toyed with their food. "Well, George, things can only get better now. I think the scrub tick outbreak is over."

"I'm glad we didn't let them win. There won't be any scrub ticks around for a while." George emitted a wearied sigh.

Jill was puzzled about the changes in them and wondered what had happened. She didn't have to wonder long. They were the stars of the next evening's television news, arrested for operating a gang of extortionists who collected protection money from businesses throughout Victoria. Anyone who resisted or didn't pay was beaten or exterminated like a scrub tick. Trying to exterminate Tony had been their downfall. He was a tick that talked.

Soft Boiled Eggs

By mid-morning the sun would be scorching, drying out the little moisture left in his wrinkled, leathery skin. Henry had once loved the hot climate. Now it sapped his energy and addled his brain. The sun hurt his eyes too. He had been told the glare would be less of a problem once the cataracts were removed. He avoided thinking about cataract surgery.

As yet, the sun was gentle, casting a yellow light over the frangipani, hibiscus and other tropical trees and shrubs in his garden. He never tired of what he called his own little bit of paradise. He gazed out at the azure water of Darwin Harbour, sparkling as if it had been dusted with diamonds. Tomorrow, the sleek forty foot yacht, Pink Horizon, would sail that azure water. There would be a crew of fit, younger men but Henry would be at the helm, the wind in his face and the taste of salt on his lips. His days of standing at the helm were numbered and he was afraid.

It was not death that scared Henry. He was afraid of what lay between now and death. He was afraid of losing his soul, one fragment at a time. Afraid of relegating Pink Horizon and all the things that made up the very core of his being to some dark abyss called "the past." So many things had become memories and memories were not enough.

His housekeeper had brought his breakfast to a small table beneath a magnolia tree. He breathed in the perfume of the tree's huge ivory coloured blooms and heard again the voice of a young woman busily digging a hole with a spade. "When we are old, Darling, we will eat breakfast beneath this tree." And they had. Now he had only the memory of Inga. He would eat alone.

"What have you made for me, Jenny?"

"Soft boiled eggs with hot buttered toast." He had known the answer. It was Friday, soft boiled eggs day. Asking was a long held habit and Henry was one to stick to habits which were pleasant.

There were two eggs in two egg cups. "Ah, Inga, my love, did you know I get to use your egg cup as well as mine?" He felt sure Inga knew this and was smiling. He carefully removed the top of an egg and added salt and pepper before dipping a finger of toast in it. He had always considered the egg cups ridiculous. White and shaped like miniature goblets, they were decorated with blue flowers. Around the rims was a pattern that looked like blue blanket stitch. It was particularly ludicrous that egg cups should be finished with blanket stitch.

Though they had agreed about most of the important things, Henry and Inga sometimes had quite different tastes and opinions about art and decor. He marvelled at how she could find beauty in the most mundane or even ugly thing. It was as if her own beauty had given her the gift of generosity towards people, objects and places less blessed.

She had accompanied him on a business trip to Singapore and had been excited and scared about a shopping spree on her own. Her face glowed with exuberance when they later met back at their hotel. She proudly showed him her purchases, shoes, handbags and a silk dress. She kept her favourite purchase till last. The egg cups. He thought them ugly but lied and said he liked them. She had stood before him, her soft green summer dress showing off her slender figure and honey coloured skin, her long ebony hair in a pony tail, her green eyes sparkling, her beauty contrasting with the humble egg cups in her hands. They had returned to Darwin on a Thursday and the soft boiled eggs tradition had begun on Friday morning.

***

Henry stood at the helm of Pink Horizon, rejoicing as her sleek hull, powered by wind filled sails, cut through the water. His love affair with sailing was just as intense as his love for Inga. He had lost none of his ardour for either. One of the crew called "The wind's perfect for the spinnaker. Should we hoist it, Henry?"

"Get ready to hoist the spinnaker." Henry steered into the wind. Then, gripped by a crushing pain, he gasped for breath and clutched his chest. He lost consciousness as he slumped forward over the tiller. There was frantic activity as the crew scrambled to help him and to control the yacht at the same time.

Henry survived the first heart attack and the race to hospital by water police and ambulance. In fact, he rallied long enough for his daughter and sons to come to his bedside. He didn't survive the second heart attack a few days later. His last words were something about eating soft boiled eggs beneath a magnolia tree. He was smiling.

 # The Tailor and the Spiders 

Way outback in the middle of nowhere, there once lived a tailor and two spiders, one purple, the other orange. All day long, the spiders made silky threads in hues of purple and orange. At night, they rested.

The tailor, whose name was Nimblefingers, wove the thread into cloth with two long golden knitting needles. Each day he toiled for many hours, the golden needles going click clack, click clack all the while. In autumn, he sometimes wove orange leaves into the cloth. Sometimes he wove purple flowers.

When Nimblefingers had enough cloth, he cut it into shapes, using big golden scissors. Snip, snip, snip. Then he joined the pieces together with a golden darning needle and orange and purple thread. He made all kinds of clothes; jackets, shirts, trousers, skirts, dresses and many other things. These clothes were wondrously warm in winter and cool in summer. At night, Nimblefingers rested.

Nimblefingers became famous throughout the land. He was even famous in other lands. Prime Ministers and other important people made long journeys with large sums of money to purchase the clothes. Nimblefingers told them, "My fee is but a few dollars but you must promise to do three good deeds every month for the rest of your life." There were many who would not make this promise and so they left empty handed.

On the other side of the land, lived a greedy man known as Layabout. When he heard about Nimblefingers, the two spiders and the silky thread, he travelled across the land for many days. At night, he rested.

He drew near Nimblefinger's house and hid behind a gum tree until night. Then he hurried to a window and peered inside. The moon was shining through the window and Layabout could see Nimblefingers fast asleep in bed. Snore, snore, snore. The spiders' eyes were closed as they hung side by side from the ceiling.

Layabout crept inside. Creep, creep, creep. He grabbed Orange spider and tried to put it in his pocket. Orange spider squealed very loudly. Squeeaal, squeeaal. Purple spider woke and gave Layabout a poke with a golden knitting needle. Layabout dropped Orange spider and ran off to hide behind the gum tree.

The next night, he came creeping back. Creep, creep, creep. He reached for Purple spider but Orange spider heard and pricked him with the golden darning needle. Layabout ran off and hid behind the gum tree. He came creeping back the next night. Creep, creep, creep.

This time, the spiders just pretended to be asleep. They spun their silken threads of orange and purple and tied Layabout up so that he couldn't move. Layabout howled, "Let me go! Let me go!" Nimblefingers woke up and cut off Layabout's legs with the golden scissors. Snip, snip, snip, snip.

Then Layabout was sorry for what he had done. "Pleeaase Nimblefingers, sew my legs on!"

Nimblefingers replied, "I will sew your legs on but only if you agree to them being sewn on backwards, that you never steal again and that you stay here and help me with my work."

Layabout said, "Yes. Yes. Yes." Nimblefingers used the golden darning needle and orange and purple threads to sew his legs on backwards. For ever after, Layabout made a shuffling noise when he walked. Shhuffle, shhuffle, shhuffle. Nimblefingers, Orange spider, Purple spider and

Layabout worked together for many years until, one by one, they died of old age. Since that time, such wondrous clothes have never again been seen in all the land.

33

Beyond Bonegilla

41 Gertrude Street,
Fitzroy.
1/8/1950.

Dear Traudi,

I wish that you will be not upset that I write letter to you. I know you a small time from the ship and Bonegilla. I much like your company.

Apology for not so goot English. Very much I like to learn better English. Also your langwich. For now, just my not so goot English.

The railway work is hard but goot and plenty fresh air. Every week I haf pay. This is very goot. The boss a goot man. The oder men are not full kind but I manage. I am happy to haf work and money and liv free!

I haf small room to liv and meals. I like best food from Czechoslovakia but cannot haf. I do not like the roast sheep but is better than starfing in Czechoslovakia.

I am sad that you are far away. I wish that I talk with you and your brothers. Most, I wish I talk with you. Greetings to your brothers. Also, they are my brothers. I haf not so goot frends here. Some Australians haf not heard of Czechoslovakia. At Bonegilla, everyone haf same story. But I thanks Got every day that I am here. Free!

Here is cold like Bonegilla. The river is small but nice. I wish to fish. I haf been to the beach at Saint Kilda. It is long from here. In sommer, I will swim. I haf never swim in the sea. There is much I wish to do.

Sorrow for my country and family and frends stays in my heart but my body is strong. I hope also you are strong. I wish the sadness in your heart lets you to smile. I wish to se you smile again.

I wish much for you to write letter to me even that I am not deserf. Please, no worry if you are bisy or haf no interest.

Your frend for ever,

Jaraslov Kruzynski.

Royal hotel,
Main Street,
Benalla.
24/9/1950.

Dear Jaraslov,

First I say your letter it did not upset me. I am pleased to be hearing vom you.

There have been much changes on my life. Already I am working at Royal Hotel for two months. I do much things, clean, cook, bring meals, work in bar. It is sometimes hard but good. I meet much people and learn to laugh. Mrs Fitzsimmons, my boss, she learns me English. I have also a small room. I think the sadness for my country is not so big.

Your letter, it came when I was already not at Bonegilla. It was again posted so it had another journey and much time before I have it. I am pleased you have good job and get some money. I also thank God that my brothers and I also can live free with good bed and food. I hope my mother and father in Heaven know that we are safe.

I am lonely for my brothers. Josef, he is in Adelaide. Also Hannas works in a forest in New South Wales. I cried much when they go. I worry that I never see them again but this thinking is not good. I have one letter from Josef, in Deutch! It made me much happy and excited. He is fit. I know Hannas also will write.

Also I am lonely for a few persons vom Bonegilla. I speak of them in my prayer.

A different language is not so easy. I read much and ask much questions. Jaraslov, your knowing of English is now bigger.

Here the weather is soon warm. I feel strange that Berlin is soon cold. I try not to think on such things. I have also never swim in sea. I have been invited to swim in the river. It does not look clean.

I will wait for your next letter,

Your friend,

Traudi Baumgartner.

41 Gertrude Street,
Fitzroy.
20/10/1950.

Dear Traudi,

I sleep a lot on the bus journey back to Melbourne. I don't mind I am sleepy. I am very happy that I see you and that you are happy to see me.

I wish you like the photos I send. I am so happy I have a photo of you. I look it many times every day.

I ask you very big question but I wish that I know the answer soon. Each day I think much from you. Each Thursday night I go to English class. In the future, not far, I work again as engineer and have better money for a home. I wish you be happy in this home with me. Vladimir from Bonegilla is working with me for two weeks already. We talk about Bonegilla and play cards. He is a good man and lonely for his home country like me. We talk together will we ever see our old countrys one time again but think it is all changed. Vladimir is now like a brother for me like your Hannas and Josef. I ask God my brother come to Australia but he feels much for our mother and father.

I visit botanical gardens on Saturday. Interesting flowers and trees. Different from Czechoslovakia. The sun was warm and many persons rested on the grass. I also had a short sleep on the grass!

Vladimir knows a cafe in Saint Kilda where there is much European food. It is called The Shirazez and the owners help many people from Europe. We wish to go there one day. Also in Saint Kilda are many cake shops. I much enjoy cakes.

I wish one day go with you to the Zoo to see Koala. I wish that you be here, Traudi.

I finish now and send you great love,

Jaroslov.

Royal Hotel,
Main Street,
Benalla.
7/11/1950.

My dear Jaroslov,

I am, of course, happy to be receiving your letter. Thank you for the photos. I have placed your photo in my bible.

Your visit was big surprise! It made me very happy. I think on you many times every day.

I have much exciting news. I will be travelling to Melbourne on November 16th. I write to Queen Victoria Hospital for Women to work as assistant in pathology and have meeting on November 17th. If I am being lucky, they like me and I come to live and work in Melbourne. When my English speaking is better, I like to study for pathologist. In the moment, I have much to think on and to do.

In Melbourne, I stay at Porters Hotel in Swanston Street. I hope we might meet when your work is finished. I am too much excited!

I will be a small bit sorry to leave Benalla. Bonegilla is not so far and that is the place where we start our new life.

Mrs Fitszimmons is also excited. She helps me sew a new dress for the meeting. I will be sorry to leave her because she has been so kind. A little like my mother.

I have not answered your big question but I have not been forgetting. It is important question and it must have proper thought and proper answer. I will have answer when I come to Melbourne.

I must write letters to Josef and Hanna. In my heart, I know they will be happy I go to Melbourne.

Love from,

Traudi.

Gertrude Street,
Fitzroy.
20/11/1950.

Darling Traudi,

I am so full with happy my heart flows over. You will soon be here in Melbourne to liv!

I write letter to Josef and also to Hannas to ask that I marry you. I know they will agree on this. They are like my brothers also.

Tomorrow, I go with Vladimir to Saint Kilda to have small celebration. Maybe we eat stroganoff and afterwards cake.

I find good tailors in Flinders Lane and will get jacket and trousers for our wedding. I must also be getting shoes and shirt.

My teacher says I learn English well so next year I study to be Engineer. I am angry I must do this because I am already Engineer. Anger does not help so I do it. I will earn more money as Engineer and maybe we one day haf our own house.

I am very glad I come to this country and meet you. We will make good life together.

Please write a letter to me soon.

Much love,

Jarasalov.

Royal Hotel
Main Street
Benalla.
30/11/1950.

Dear Jarasolov,

I write this letter with great sadness and beg of you to try to understand my situation. My brothers say I must not marry you because of your Gypsy blood.

Who is a Gypsy? A human being! Maybe it would be better if you did not tell them that your grandparents were Gypsies but I do not critic you for being honest. Perhaps it is really honour to have such ancestors. That your grandparents were without education and you are engineer proofs that you are a good and clever man. I tell this Josef and Hannas when they visit me but they say they will not have their sister married to a Gypsy.

My brothers say they will not know me if I marry you. I have no other family in the world. Whatever decision I take, I will be unhappy and others too. I have decided to do as my brothers wish.

We must both make a good life for ourselves in this country. I am sure I am already a better person from knowing you. I wish you good things for the future.

Traudi.

14 Glenburn Rd
Henly
South Australia.
14/9/1980.

Dear Traudi,

What a coincidence that we should both be dining at the same cafe in Glenelg on the same day! I was truly delighted to see you and it was a pleasure to meet your daughter, Anna and little Imogen. You a grandmother! I must say a young looking grandmother.

I hope you enjoyed the remainder of your time here in Adelaide. It is, of course, not as big as Melbourne but has lots to see.

In your last letter to me all those years ago, you said that we must do our best to make a good life here in this country. At first, I was angry and hurt by your decision but then I realized you really had no choice. I feel I have made a good life even though I have been unlucky in love and have divorced twice. I have a son who lives here in Adelaide with his mother.

Who would have thought that I would one day have my own engineering firm? It is doing very well and there is plenty of work. I told you about my little yacht and how much I love sailing.

More importantly, I have found some great friends. Did I tell you that Vladimir is working for me? He has been loyal and, at times, has provided much comfort.

Ten years ago, my father died and my mother the year after. I longed to see them before they died but it wasn't to be. Three years ago, my brother, using various means, came to Australia. We are still getting to know each other.

Traudi, we didn't have much time to talk but I am glad that we exchanged addresses. I hope that we might keep in touch. Perhaps I can one day teach you to sail.

Your friend,

Jaraslov.

21 Grovedale Street,
Kew
Victoria.
26/9/1980.

Dear Jaraslov,

Meeting with you was a lovely surprise! I am sorry that we didn't have more time to talk. We have, no doubt, changed greatly over the years but, in essence, you seem to be the same Jaraslov I knew so long ago.

Anna was delighted to meet someone who had been in Bonegilla with me and her uncles. I confess that I had never told her about you. When I told her about your Gypsy ancestor, she was even more impressed. She says she will invite you to dinner with her husband and little Imogen. I hope you will accept. I do miss Anna now that she lives in Adelaide but I can at least visit her from time to time.

I am sure you would like my son, Christian and my other daughter, Maria. They have all turned out well and I am proud of them. After Gunter's death, I went back to work and the children had to care for themselves a lot of the time. Anna was fourteen, Christian thirteen and Maria only eleven. My brothers lived far away and had their own families by then.

Gunter was a good man but he suffered many losses before he came to Australia. He carried much bitterness in his heart and became a harsh person. When he became ill, he lost his will. In a way, it was a blessing the end came swiftly for him. Josef and Hannas never knew how harsh Gunter had grown. However, it does no good to dwell on such matters.

I hope that we might be able to stay in touch. Perhaps a grandmother could learn to sail! We could speak about it next time I visit Anna. You must visit me if you are in Melbourne. My telephone number is (03) 801275.

Yours in friendship,

Traudi.

Puerwook

Long long ago, way out back in the middle of nowhere, there was a place called Puerwook. The folk who lived in Puerwook, and for some distance beyond, were not rich but they were contented. They weren't spared the usual hardships and tragedies that most folk face. Children were left motherless when mothers died from a chill; mothers were left childless when babies were accidently rolled on in bed and fathers were crippled when horses trampled on them. There were seasons of too much rain and floods and seasons of bush fires and too little rain.

There were often other difficulties like a shortage of butter churns or good quality boots. There were scones that didn't rise, hens that didn't lay eggs and cows that had no milk. The folk of Puerwook remained cheerful. You see, not far away, there was a black stump with magical powers. Whenever someone was troubled, they would go to the black stump. Some folk sat on it, others leaned on it and others merely put their ear to it. If they were very quiet, sure enough they would leave knowing just what to do.

There were just three rules, which everyone knew, though no one remembered being told. They were not to come with bad thoughts; they must not damage the black stump and they must not come back until three days had passed.

One day early in March, there was a high pitched wailing in the main street. Everyone stopped what they were doing and hurried to see what was happening.

"It's gone, clean gone! Ohhhh! Ohhhh! It's gone!" Mrs Enoon, a farmer's wife was wailing and spluttering and making no sense at all. Even her husband couldn't get any sense out of her. She just kept wailing, "Ohhh, Ohhh! It's gone!"

At last, her husband said, "I will go to the black stump to find out what to do."

Mrs Enoon wailed even louder, "Ohhh, ohhh! It's gone! The black stump is gone!"

And so it was. There was just a big hole in the ground where it once stood. Word soon spread and the people of Puerwook mourned. Even folk who lived far away from the middle of nowhere mourned.

Three search parties were set up. Mrs Enoon insisted on going with a search party so her husband stayed at home to receive reports.

At the end of the first day, one search party reported seeing some squashed spinnafex. At the end of the second day, another search party reported seeing a piece of blackened wood.

On the third day, Mrs Enoon's search party heard the sound of an axe coming from a gully. Very soon, deep in the gully, they came upon the black stump. Standing before it, was a man with a big axe. He had already chopped some bits off it.

"Who are you and what are you doing?" demanded Mrs Enoon.

"I'm Wollefdab and I'm chopping up this useless black stump for firewood," the man replied.

"What do mean by useless?" said Mrs Enoon.

"I've waited three days and it has told me nothing."

A man in the search party cried out, "You stole it. Give it back!"

Wollefdab lifted his axe. "I will not give it back. I will do what I like with it!"

The search party surrounded Wollefdab and overpowered him. Then Mrs Enoon split him in two with his own axe.

There was much rejoicing as the black stump was returned to its former place. Once again, folk from round about came to it when they were troubled.

The climate grew hotter and drier and, eventually, all the folk of Puerwook moved to the coast. The town no longer exists but, somewhere way out back in the middle of nowhere, there is a black stump. These days, no one knows where it is. If ever you come upon it, remember that, providing you obey the rules, it will help you with your troubles.

That First Summer

I cannot for my soul remember when I last saw you. I'm sure two months or more have passed. I saw you often that first summer. You looked strong and energetic, your face was tanned, your smiling eyes kind and gentle. I sometimes saw you sitting in your chair; sometimes digging in the garden and sometimes patting Spot. When I reached out to touch you, there was nothing beneath my hand. Then my sadness knew no end.

I cannot for my soul remember when I last felt your touch. That first summer, I felt you gently brush my shoulder; your soft kiss on my cheek and your closeness as you snuggled next to me on the couch. At night, during autumn and winter, I felt you tuck the blankets around my body. My heart froze with loneliness when I discovered the emptiness of my bed.

I cannot for my soul remember when I last heard your voice. I heard you often that first summer. At times, you would call me from another room or I would hear you laughing at Spot. I smiled with happiness when I heard you singing. I have never stopped loving your tuneless voice. I looked for you, only to be mocked by silence. The silence then swallowed my weeping for my despair was beyond utterance. My spirit was imprisoned in a place without light when I heard you open the front door but no one stepped into the house.

Some say that I am learning to live without you. In truth, I am learning to live with your absence. There is an unquenched yearning that still burns hotly inside me. Perhaps tomorrow, I will breathe in the familiar smell of you as I did that first summer.

I Kept Your First Shoes

I kept your first shoes. I'm sentimental that way. They are scuffed and a buckle is loose, but I might have them painted in gold and hang them on a wall. I never imagined such tiny feet would one day carry you fast as a hare on the running track. There's a pair of rubber thongs discarded by the front door. I don't plan to hang them on a wall.

You kept Polly Dolly. Her yellow hair has faded a bit but her rag face still smiles from a shelf in your room. She was the one who broke and lost things and danced with the other toys while you slept. She watched you grow, thrive and achieve. Then she watched illness sap your strength, leaving you like a wilted flower. Polly Dolly knows the things you've told no one.

I kept a curl snipped from your head when you were barely walking. At Little Aths, they all cheered for the girl with "spaghetti hair". You never got to compete in the Olympic Games and now you spend hours, it seems, straightening your hair with a heated wand.

You kept your flower girl dress. You looked like a princess that day. At the wedding breakfast, someone put a cushion on your chair so that you could reach the table. These days, you rarely wear anything other than pyjamas.

I kept piles of your stuff from school. You never mastered the spelling game but scored "A" for most other things. That was until brain fog and exhaustion hit you. In spite of that, you struggled on and even did well at Uni for a while. Who knows, you might someday complete your studies.

You kept your medals and trophies. They're in a box under your bed where you've stashed your starting blocks. My tears were bitter sweet the day you packed them away. You had, at last, accepted that you would never again run swift as a hare.

I kept your first shoes.

Footsteps

Elijah was scared of being alone in the dark. The light switch was on the other side of the room. He could get out of bed and turn it on but there could be a bad person hiding in the corner. He hugged his teddy bear and pulled the scratchy blanket over his head.

He wished his mother was there. When she tucked him into bed, she'd said, "Be a good boy and wait here. When I come back, I will bring you something to eat." She smelled of soap and Elijah thought she had probably left her perfume at the house. He wanted something to eat right then. He was hungry. He listened to her soft footsteps in the corridor.

Their room was on the second floor. Elijah didn't like it but his mother had said, "Look, we've got our own bathroom." She had smiled but her face was sad.

There was no elevator, just stairs at the end of the corridor. Elijah listened as heavy footsteps ascended the stairs. The noise echoed in the stairwell. Elijah lay still and tried not to breathe loudly. Could his father know they were here? Would he know exactly what room? The footsteps stopped before they reached his door, and some other door slammed.

He fell asleep for a while then woke. He was still alone. His mother wasn't there. He was hungrier now. Maybe his mother wouldn't come back. She had left his father. If she could do that, she could leave him. He began to cry and then remembered why she had left his father. She was tired of being punched. Elijah had never punched her and he always tried to be good. Surely she wouldn't leave him.

He heard more footsteps. This time they went right past his door. He was very hungry. He heard a mouse scuffling in the ceiling and wondered if it was hungry. His mother was afraid of mice, he wasn't.

He slept again until the smell of hot meat pie woke him. This time, he hadn't heard his mother's soft footsteps. He sat on the edge of the bed and ate the meat pie. Afterwards, his mother cleaned his face with a tissue. She hugged him, saying, "You're a good boy. I love you. There's an old couch in a room at the back of the pie shop. Tomorrow, you can sleep there while I work." Now Elijah was sure she wouldn't leave him like she had left his father.

The Queen of the Golden Mountain

Long ago, a rich gold miner lived in a gold mansion in a town not far from his gold mines. There were many servants to care for him, his wife and four daughters who were famous for their beauty.

Early one summer, his wife gave birth to their fifth daughter whom they named "Emerald" because of her green eyes. She was fair to look upon and grew into a pleasant and obedient child, but there was a secret known only to her mother and a midwife who had been present at the birth. On the back of Emerald's left shoulder, there was a round purple birth mark. The midwife had been sworn to secrecy because it was believed that such a mark was a sign that the child had been touched by evil and must be killed.

The midwife, who was also a nursemaid, was a cruel and greedy woman who demanded more and more to keep quiet. She often slapped Emerald for no good reason. When Emerald was twelve years old, she accidently spilled a bowl of broth on the midwife's best dress and ruined it. The midwife flew into a rage and, out of spite, told the gold miner about the birth mark.

The gold miner immediately had Emerald brought before him and examined her left shoulder. He saw the birth mark and his heart was broken. "I love this daughter very much," he said, "but she must be executed because she is a witch." On hearing this, Emerald's mother took her to a nearby forest. "You must remain hidden here and I will bring you food and water when I can." She left some bread, biscuits and water.

The gold miner sent out a search party and Emerald went deeper into the forest where even her mother couldn't find her. At night, she slept under a log. When her food and water were almost gone, she cried in despair.

Just then, a large grey kangaroo came by. "Why do you cry?" she asked. Emerald told her story. "I will take you to a bunyip that will help you but first you must stay with me for five days and massage my neck which I have injured. I will show you all the fruits of the forest that you can eat."

Emerald did as she was asked, and then she and the kangaroo journeyed for five days. On the sixth day, they came to a dark cave where the bunyip lived. She spoke very gruffly."Why have you come here?"

Emerald replied, "Mrs Bunyip, I mean you no harm and have come to ask for your help." Then she told the bunyip her story.

Mrs Bunyip said, "First you must prove that you are not a witch. You must care for my sick husband and if you can make him well I will know that you are not a witch and you are worthy of help."

Emerald cared for the sick bunyip husband who lay close to death deep inside the cave. She fashioned a container from bark and brought fresh water from a stream. She gathered nuts, grass and leaves, broke them into small pieces and put them in the bunyip husband's mouth, but he was too weak to eat more than a few mouthfuls at one time. After many months, the bunyip's husband had improved only a little. Displeased, Mrs Bunyip said," You have not proved that you are not a witch so I must kill you."

Emerald pleaded with her. "Your husband is not cured but he is a little stronger. Please give me more time." Mrs Bunyip eventually agreed.

It was three years before Mrs Bunyip's husband was cured and moved outside the cave. She was well pleased. She said, "You have proved you are not a witch and no evil spirit lives in you. I will remove the mark from your shoulder but first you must bring me a feather plucked from the breast of a magpie, a quill plucked from a porcupine, the shed skin of a snake and the egg of a goanna."

Emerald went out to gather these things. She came upon a magpie and her three young ones warbling in a tree. It laughed at Emerald's request. "Foolish girl, whatever would you do with a feather from my breast?" Just the same, it plucked a feather from its breast and gave it to Emerald who thanked it and continued on her way.

Next she came upon a porcupine curled up under a log. It said,"No! You cannot have one of my quills! I need them all to protect my children." When she heard Emerald's story, she allowed an old, loose quill to be plucked from her back. Then she showed Emerald where a shed snake skin lay.

On the third day, Emerald came upon the nest of a goanna. Two large goannas were guarding it. They agreed to trade an egg which was not quite perfect for one hundred witchetty grubs. It took Emerald many days to find the grubs but the goannas were pleased and happily gave her the egg.

The bunyip used the snake skin, the feather and the porcupine quill to make a necklace which she told Emerald to wear for three days and three nights. Then she rubbed the yolk of the goanna egg onto the birthmark. The next morning, there was no trace of the mark.

The bunyip sent a black cockatoo to find the grey kangaroo and asked it to take Emerald back to her home. After many days, they arrived at the golden mansion, Emerald wearing a cloak made from grass. Her family were at first afraid, but she showed them her left shoulder and then they believed she was not a witch and welcomed her.

That night, there was a fierce thunderstorm and the midwife was struck by a bolt of lightning. She died instantly.

Emerald's father ordered his workers to build her a mansion on a mountain covered with rocks of gold. Not long after, the King, upon hearing Emerald's story, sent his son, the Prince, to visit. The Prince and Emerald fell in love and were married, choosing to live in the mansion on the mountain of gold instead of a palace. The King grew old and died and the Prince inherited the throne but he refused to live anywhere else. From thenceforth, Emerald was known as the Queen of the Golden Mountain.

Tension Could Kill A Man

Riley washed the last piece of pizza down with a few swigs of beer from a bottle sitting on the crowded coffee table. Now that his belly was full, he felt a bit drowsy. He leaned back against the worn brown velour couch. He'd have to meet Davo tomorrow to discuss the final plans for the next job.

There was knocking at the front door. It was 10pm and Riley wasn't expecting anyone this late. He looked through the peep hole. Cops! He should have known.

Riley had to act fast. If he didn't open the door, they'd go round the back then return and smash the door down. Jesus! There might be a couple of them already round the back. He grabbed his wallet off the coffee table, no time for anything else. Hurrying out the back door, he didn't check if cops were in the back yard. If they were there, they'd have seen him anyway.

He put one foot on a knee high ledge on the paling fence and hoisted himself over the top, landing in the neighbour's back yard. Crouching low, he scurried along by the fence hoping no one would look out a window. A beam of torch light shone through a crack in the fence. He was breathing hard. Hard enough to be heard by a cop coming close by. He crept forward until he reached a small shrub and hid behind it. They would search the neighbouring properties soon. He needed to think of something; make a plan.

Riley waited there, crouching in the dark for what seemed like hours but was probably minutes. He could hear no one. He peered through a knot hole in the fence.

There was no torch light. They'd be breaking down his front door.

He had two choices. He could keep leaping over back fences until he was well away and risk being seen from a window or being bitten from a dog. It would also be a noisy business. The other option was to scale the fence between him and the front yard and make a dash for it along the street.

He chose the second option. Still crouching, he darted to the next fence. It also had a knee high ledge. He put his left foot on it and prepared to hoist his right leg up. The ledge gave way with a loud crack. Riley could either drop back to the ground or go over the top. He went over the top.

Now he was on the street running hard. His right ankle was hurting badly. He must have twisted it. He tried to ignore the pain. There were footsteps behind him. He didn't look back. He had to outrun them. He might be able to hide somewhere; dart behind something in the darkness.

Ahead, he made out the shape of a rubbish skip standing on the side of the street. He could hear the cops still on his tail. One called out, "Riley, it's no use. Stop where you are."

"Holy shit," he thought, "Are they planning to shoot me?" Perspiration dripped from his forehead and down his back but he hardly noticed.

He clambered over the side of the skip. It was full of garden waste, old bricks and bits of timber. Stifling a moan, Riley flattened himself amongst the rubbish. The pain in his ankle was excruciating and was extending up his leg.

He peeked over the side of the skip just as two panting cops ran past. Then he spotted a police car approaching slowly. Ducking back down, Riley listened. The police car passed. He decided to wait a minute or two then scramble out of the tip and try to make his way to a train station, though he might have to crawl, judging by the pain in his ankle and leg.

There were no footsteps; no cars. Time to go. It was easy to swing over the side of the skip and drop to the ground. Then Riley's right leg crumpled beneath him. He fell hard, his face in the gutter.

Riley woke with a start, his face on the coffee table, his right leg twisted awkwardly beneath it. He took a few moments to recognize his surroundings. "That's it," he said to himself. "Davo will have to find someone else to drive the getaway car. Just thinking about it is giving me nightmares. All this tension could kill a man."

That's All That Mattered

"Stop crying. It helps nothing." Natasha's mother's words and the message they carried were imprinted on her mind. One must be strong, keep going and never give up regardless of difficulties. Natasha had followed that creed all her life. She learned how to be strong and in control. Somewhere along the way, she had forgotten how to cry.

Her parents had known great hardship. They had fled from war torn Yugoslavia, firstly to Austria and then to Australia, arriving with little more than the clothes they wore. They toiled in grimy Sydney factories and made a home for themselves in a back street of Parramatta. When Natasha was born, her mother resigned from her job, leaving them to live on one wage.

Natasha's knowledge of those years was limited. Her mother rarely spoke of the difficulties. If questioned, she would say "It was not easy but, thanks God, we had a house, a bed and food."

Natasha didn't remember her Dad. He died when she was three years old and so she knew him only as a smiling face in photos and as an unseen person in a grave her mother took her to visit at regular intervals. Her mother had kept his best blue shirt hanging in the wardrobe and his wedding ring in her purse. She often said "He was a good man." If she wept at all, it was in private. Natasha has never witnessed it.

Somehow Natasha's mother managed by working in factories and cleaning houses. Natasha was left in the care of neighbours and, later, on her own. Mother and daughter had a close bond, supporting and protecting each other, sharing the good times and the bad. In time, they became known as two strong, independent women.

Now, all that had changed. Her mother's illness had been merciless, killing her in spite of the best efforts of her medical team. Natasha was alone and devastated. A suffocating cloud of grief descended upon he. Her body felt as though it was weighted with heavy chains. She did all the right things; arranged the funeral and the burial and thanked those who offered their condolences. She accepted the flowers and the dishes of food people gave her but declined any offers of help. After all, she had to be strong.

She didn't feel strong. Her mother was dead. It was a hideous word, an unthinkable truth that she wished she could hide from. Nothing would change this truth. She was powerless. Her anguish was worsened by the fact that there seemed to be no deed, no utterance by which it could be expressed.

Her friend, Rianna phoned and heard the anguish in her voice. "Come and spend some time here in Alice Springs. I could do with a bit of help in the shop now that the tourist season has started."

Natasha has been at first reluctant but finally agreed and boarded a plane to take her to the middle of Australia. It seemed like a mistake. Even the warm sunshine and the vivid colours of the red centre seemed oppressive. She watched as Aboriginal people wandered aimlessly around the streets and through the red dust. Their ill-fitting clothes hanging from their thin bodies, slumped shoulders, bowed heads and the pendulous breasts of the women seemed to be mimicking the drooping foliage of the eucalyptus trees. There was heaviness about it all that echoed the heaviness she felt inside herself.

Natasha decided she would return to Sydney as soon as she could do so without being disrespectful to Rianna.

She must wait until after the market and festival which was to be held in a few days.

The evening was warm and the park was humming with a festive air. Market stalls offered an infinite variety of wares; vendors offered food   reflecting the multi-cultural community; jugglers and flame swallowers displayed their skills. Natasha barely noticed any of it. She bore with her an emptiness which was dark, heavy and exhausting.

Then she heard a throbbing and droning sound mingled with the sound of sticks clapped against each other. She was drawn to the sound like a moth drawn to light. A group of dark skinned men played didgeridoos while others beat sticks together in time with the rhythm. People began to dance, swaying their bodies and stamping their feet. Natasha felt herself responding to the throbbing music. She began to dance. Her outstretched arms swayed with her body; her feet moved of their own accord. She had become part of the music.

The didgeridoos throbbed and droned and, for the first time since she was a small child, tears spilled from Natasha's eyes and coursed down her cheeks. Others were watching her now but she didn't care. She danced for joy. She had learned how to cry and let go of control. That's all that mattered.

Autumn Leaves

Avril was oblivious to the falling autumn leaves as she waited to be served at the outdoor cafe. There was a time when she delighted in the beauty of autumn leaves and took great pleasure in watching them change from green to yellows and rich russets, oranges and browns. A time when she would toss them into the air for the sheer joy of watching them swirl and float then fall to the ground. She would go out of her way to hear them rustle and crunch beneath her feet. Sometimes she had run barefoot through parks, dancing and twirling, feeling at peace and at one with nature.

The generous mug of coffee was strong, the way she preferred it. The eggs Benedict were just the right consistency, served with wilted spinach, hot buttered toast and slices of crispy bacon. Through dulled senses, she recognised the rich aromas and taste of this feast but took no comfort from it.

There was little comfort in anything these days. She hid her constant exhaustion from most people but her friend, Veronica, was more astute. Two days ago, Veronica had dropped by to return a borrowed recipe book. "You look tired and you're losing weight. Are you eating and sleeping well? Are you looking after yourself?" Her eyes were full of concern.

Avril shrugged it off. "I've stayed up late a few nights getting my accounts and things in order and I've given the garden a good overhaul." She knew her tiredness was more than that.

Veronica was never one to be fooled."Don't try hiding

things. You can always talk to me."

"I don't know what I'd talk about but I do know I don't want to talk about it now." Even Veronica's familiar warm, matronly presence brought no comfort.

Since Veronica's visit, Avril had tried to eat better, to eat three meals a day, to eat all the meal instead of scattering most of it in the garden for the birds. She ate the last of the bacon without being aware of the taste.

She *was* aware of the warm sun on her face, though her soul felt cold. There was an hour before her appointment so she decided to order more coffee and sit a while. She could at least tell Veronica she was trying to look after herself by boosting her Vit D levels.

A newspaper lay on the next table. Avril took it and idly scanned the headlines. She rarely read a newspaper these days; they seemed to be full of doom and gloom. She turned to the horoscope page even though she didn't believe in such mumbo jumbo. There was her sign, Libra. *You are feeling confused right now. You have a sense of disconnection from those around you. This is distressing but try not to worry because there will soon be a positive change.* The horoscope guru sure knew how she was and knew the essence of her, but telling her what she already knew was pointless. As for a "positive change", she didn't see how that would happen. She didn't believe in miracles either.

Dr Matt Greenbrae was a quietly spoken, pleasant and kindly fellow. His shirt strained over his ample girth as he sat in his big brown leather chair. His wiry grey beard was neatly trimmed. Frizzy grey hair surrounded the yarmulke on top of his head. Avril wondered if the collective sorrow and mourning for the persecution and murder of his forbears had been what led him to take up psychiatry. It was not a question she would ask him.

Sitting opposite him in a similar chair, she feared Matt was displeased with her. "It's over two years since Phillip passed away and your mood hasn't shown any sign of improving. We've talked about this before and I really think it's time you tried some medication. To avoid side effects, you could begin with a very small dose, though it will take longer before you feel any real benefit."

Avril didn't want medication. "Matt, it's not so much the loss of my husband. It's just that I feel I don't fit in anywhere. I don't see how medication will help."

Matt wrote her a prescription anyway. Avril put it in her handbag without any intention of having it filled. She made another appointment but feared that he wouldn't want to see her if she didn't take medication.

She walked along the river bank, passing a man and woman sharing a picnic lunch in the sunshine. They laughed as they poured coffee from a flask. Loneliness gripped her like a vice and she wondered if the ability to engage with others had been lost to her forever. She wondered if she would one day grow used to being imprisoned inside an invisible bubble.

She encountered no other people as she walked further. Then, uncaring about soiling her clothes, she wearily sat on the grass and looked into the water. Like most other parts of the country, the city had been inundated by an unusual amount of rain for many months. The river was a deeper shade of its usual muddy hue, as if it had taken on the murkiness of Avril's life

A crooked stick slowly drifted past on the current. Caught up against it and borne along with it, was a plastic bag. A blue plastic bag. It, too, seemed to resemble Avril. Unwanted, it had been carelessly cast aside, tossed hither and thither by the wind and now it drifted helplessly in murky water. It was held tightly against the crooked stick but that connection could be broken at any moment. Her own few connections with other people felt just as tenuous. In fact, she felt no connection at all with most people.

It had started with Phillip's long illness. The doctors had done their best but there was no cure. He gradually grew frailer. Avril gave up her work and career to care for him. She missed her clients and lost contact with her colleagues. Friends stopped visiting or phoning. Perhaps they found Phillip's illness too confronting .Phillip deteriorated further and she stopped going to her social activities. Her daughter, Tessa, fell in love with a young man and left home to live with him. She had never deserted her parents but was busy with her own life and career. Avril held no resentment about this.

She had mourned long before Phillip died. Mourned for the man he once was and for the things he and she might have done. She missed him now just as keenly as she did in those first months following his death but felt that his spirit was always close by. For this she was immensely thankful.

Why couldn't Matt understand that she was not still struggling with the loss of Phillip, it was the loss of connection with other people?

The blue plastic bag had drifted away from the crooked stick and was further downstream. It was partly submerged and Avril wondered how long it would be before it sunk to the muddy riverbed, no longer at the mercy of wind or rain or river current. She could easily slip into the water and sink to the muddy bottom just like the plastic bag. Then there would be no need for connections to others. The invisible bubble would worry her no more.

No. To drown herself, to end it all would not be fair to Tessa. It would cause her unbearable pain. Veronica would also suffer. Avril remembered it was the first Friday of the month, the day Tessa and her partner, Jamie, came for dinner. She would need to get a few cooking ingredients on her way home.

She spiced the pumpkin soup with fresh ginger and added a good lashing of whisky to the beef stroganoff then made sticky date pudding with caramel sauce. She had lost none of her excellent cooking skills but her actions were without joy. She didn't savour the rich aromas. She didn't sample the pumpkin soup as she stirred it; she didn't sample the stroganoff simmering on the stove top and she didn't dip her finger in the caramel sauce.

Tessa and Jamie arrived early, bringing a large bunch of perfumed roses. "Oh, thank you. They are beautiful." Despite her exhaustion and numbed feelings, Avril was deeply conscious of what a good, wholesome couple they were. She felt blessed by their presence. As she prepared to serve the meal, she noticed that Tessa seemed to be glowing with health.

"Will you pour, Jamie?" She fetched a bottle of wine from the refrigerator.

"I'm not drinking alcohol, Mum," Tessa called.

"Why not Darling? It's your favourite."

Jamie and Tessa looked at each other and grinned. "You might as well tell her," Jamie said.

"What is it, Tessa? Is something wrong? Are you on some kind of diet?" Avril was alarmed.

"I'm having a baby. You're going to be a grandmother."

The meal was forgotten for a while as they hugged, kissed and cried, all at the same time. Somewhere inside her, Avril felt tiny stirrings of joy, just as Tessa would feel the stirrings of the new life she and Jamie had created.

Avril was concerned about the alcohol in the stroganoff but Tessa said alcohol in cooking didn't matter. For the rest of the evening, the conversation centred round the baby. Tessa served a second helping of sticky date pudding for Jamie. "We hope you will be able to help us, Mum. With babysitting and other things. There's so much we don't know and you've already been there and you've helped out with lots of other babies and kids."

Jamie butted in, "But we don't want to burden you, to be a nuisance."

"Oh, I want to help. I simply must help! In fact, I demand to help!" There were tears in her eyes as she laughed. It was not the first time she had laughed this evening, but only that morning, she had wondered if she would ever be able to laugh again.

Later, as Avril took a shower and prepared for bed, she felt a little lightheaded. She had drunk Tessa's share of wine then a little more but she didn't think it was alcohol that was affecting her. She slid between the sheets and turned off the bedside lamp. For the first time in a long while, instead of a mantle of empty exhaustion, a feeling of contentment descended upon her. Tomorrow, she would walk bare foot through autumn leaves.

Moonlight

The prison cell walls were a drab grey, and dirty. High up in one corner, there was a blood coloured stain. Emma wondered about it. Had a former occupant stolen a bit of wire coat hanger from the laundry? Had she hidden it in her bra? Had she sharpened it to a point by rubbing it on the metal bed frame? Had she then slit her wrist with it?

Emma imagined the warm red blood gushing out and splashing the wall. Arthur's blood had gushed out like that when she slit his throat. He had been sleeping on his back, so drunk that he didn't wake when she lifted his unshaven chin to expose his throat. The knife was very sharp, the cut swift and deep. His eyes had opened then, in terror. She had smiled at him and watched his blood gush out, spraying onto the ceiling, walls, furniture and herself.

"I'm free now, Arthur! Free!" she yelled. She watched until the red geyser dwindled to a trickle and the life had gone from his eyes.

After twenty years of brutal bashings and deprivation, she could do as she liked. "Now I can sing and dance and wear nice things. I can go to the movies and not bother to wash the dishes," she thought. As Arthur's blood soaked the mattress beneath him, Emma felt elated.

Her elation was short lived. The court ruled that she hadn't acted in self-defence because Arthur was asleep when she murdered him. She was sentenced to a thirty year prison term.

Three years passed and Emma was tired of prison life.

Tired of grey walls, concrete yards and the hot, steamy laundry where she worked every day. Tired of eating from metal plates, wearing drab prison clothes and being forever watched. Tired of standing in line and obeying orders.

Most of all, she longed to gaze upon the moon and stars. Their memory had been almost erased by the darkness of the prison cell where she spent her nights. Tomorrow, she would face the court once again to appeal her sentence. It would probably be as futile as her last two appeals. Her life was worthless. She should have slit her own throat instead of Arthur's. She wondered if she could hide a bit of a wire coat hanger in her bra.

That night, as she lay on her hard bed, Emma dreamed she was running, free as the wind, on a beach. The ocean glistened in the light of a million stars and a full moon. Under her feet, she felt the cool dampness of soft sand. A gentle sea breeze kissed her face and salt flavoured her lips. A long yellow silk dress swirled around her legs as they carried her further and further along the endless shoreline. She felt that she could run for ever. Run for joy.

The court hearing was shorter than the other times. Emma thought she was still dreaming when the verdict was announced. There had been a mistake. Then her Lawyer said, "You're free! "

Journalists jostled each other as she was whisked from the court. "What will you do now, Emma?"

"Run barefoot on a beach in the moonlight." But she would first need to find a yellow silk dress.

A Cup of Tea

The atmosphere in the crowded auction room was stuffy, and electrified. There was a low drone of voices as greetings were exchanged and would be buyers eyed each other with suspicion. They had examined the goods and reckoned their worth. Next would come the contest to outbid each other for the object or objects of their desire.

Eileen was interested in only one thing. Lot 265, a white porcelain tea set decorated with violets. It was just like the one her mother once used when she entertained important people at tea parties. She had kept the one remaining cup at the back of a cupboard, hidden from Ernest. She thought about how Ernest would have scoffed at her now. She could hear him say "You are full of sentimental crap!" Well, she was rid of him. She had suffered his cheating for far too long. She had no need for men in her life.

"Hello Eileen."

Each time she saw him she was more aware of his attractiveness and his smiling eyes. "Jordan, we meet again."

The auction had started they stood silently side by side. Eileen guessed he was looking for stock for his shop, The Village Antiques. She had bought several things from the shop and had been well pleased with them. They were expensive but she thought that Jordan had given her a fair deal. He had also given her some useful advice about refurbishing her cottage.

She watched him as he bid for a brass bed. *Why is he*

so darned attractive? Ernest was attractive and he was a cheat. Why does he have to stand next to me? She could move away but that would seem rude. He always stood near her when they had bumped into each other at auctions.

He was successful in his bid for the bed. She wondered what else he wanted to buy. He had once sold her a brass bed which was just perfect for her bedroom. Ernest would have hated it. Just as well they had divorced before she inherited her mother's fortune because he would have claimed his cut and she may never have been able to afford antiques.

The auctioneer called for bids for Lot 265. Eileen's pulse quickened as she waited for a few others to place their bids then she placed her own. $400, $450, $500. Eileen was determined to have it but hoped it wouldn't cost her a fortune. $550. Then she noticed that Jordan was also bidding. She was embarrassed but even more determined. The price rose higher and fewer people were bidding. Then there was just the two of them. Eileen's embarrassment turned to anger. *How dare he bid against me? He must know I want it. The arrogance of the man!* He was attractive but she hated him! She ran from the auction room with tears streaming down her face.

Two weeks later, Eileen answered a knock on her door and found Jordan standing there with a large gift wrapped box. Her voice was icy. "Oh, it's you."

He ignored her cold manner. "I hope you don't mind but I looked up your address because I've got something for you."

She was unsure of herself now. "For me?"

"Yes. Can I come in?"

Reluctantly, she showed him into the sitting room where he placed the box on a coffee table. "Open it."

She did and found it contained the violet patterned tea set, each piece carefully wrapped in tissue paper. She stared at him in amazement. He smiling eyes were teasing. "I thought you could use it to make us a cup of tea."

"I think I will do just that."Her eyes smiled back. *Perhaps this will be the first of many cups of tea. Maybe there is a place for a man in my life.*

Home for Christmas Dinner

Frenzied with excitement, the big brindle dog's tail wagged faster than helicopter blades in full flight. He watched every move as Barry gathered things for the journey.

"Settle down, Santapaws." Barry patted the dog as he walked past.

"I'm gonna miss you, Santapaws," Jan called from the kitchen where she filled a thermos flask with boiling water.

"What about me?" Barry yelled.

"You too, Love. Don't be away too long or you'll miss Christmas dinner. Remember the kids are coming."

"We'll be back in time. We'll stay just one day with Uncle Bert before heading home. We've got five days."

Barry liked to visit Uncle Bert who was lonely now that Aunt Nellie had died. The pleasure in his old eyes more than made up for the long journey. Jan had baked a Christmas cake and a tin of biscuits to take to him.

The year had been unusually wet. The rivers were full and some of the roads might be blocked. Barry was an experienced driver and his ute was reliable. "We'll be right. We won't do anything silly," he said to the dog sitting next to him in the cabin. He opened the passenger side window. Santapaws liked to hang his head out in the breeze.

Barry remembered the Christmas Eve when they found the scrawny pup by the side of a road just out of town. "He's a perfect Christmas present," Jan had said, "We'll name him Santapaws." Now they couldn't bear to part with the big goofy dog.

Uncle Bert welcomed them with a hug each. The next day, they sat together on the veranda exchanging news and talking about the old days. As the sun set, Barry said he must leave in the morning. The old man wanted him to stay longer but Barry said, "I've gotta be home for Christmas dinner."

More rain had fallen, flooding some roads. Barry had to take detours. The journey would take three days instead of two. He spent the second night in a shabby road house where dogs weren't allowed inside.

The next day was Christmas Eve. "We've gotta be home for Christmas dinner, big boy," he said as Santapaws leapt onto the passenger seat.

The last river was a roaring, muddy fury cutting through the countryside and sweeping everything in its path. The water almost reached the top of the bridge. It could be swept away at any minute. If Barry didn't cross now, it would be too late. "Hang on mate," he said as he cautiously drove forward.

Santapaws hung his head out the window and barked excitedly. Suddenly, a dead cow popped up from under the bridge and was swept downstream as if it was a fallen leaf. The dog uttered a loud yelp. Then he was gone. Out the window and into the raging water.

Too late, Barry yelled "No! You silly bloody fool!" He crossed the bridge and parked the ute on the side of the road then frantically raced along the river bank shouting, "Santapaws! Santapaws!" There was no sign of the brindle dog. He searched the river bank for hours, heedless of his sodden shoes and that he was now far from the ute. He searched until his eyes could no longer pierce the darkness of night.

Finding his way back to the ute, he wearily climbed inside. Christmas was ruined. Tears came and then sobbing as he imagined the dog's fate. Exhausted, he fell asleep.

A high pitched whining and the sound of scratching on the ute door woke him. It was Christmas morning. He opened the door as a big wet brindle dog, bleeding from a torn ear, leapt onto his lap. "Santapaws! You silly bloody fool!" Man and dog greeted each other, one with hugs and tears, the other with licks, tail wags and yelps of happiness.

"Are you badly hurt big fella?" Barry found no serious injuries. The bridge was submerged and water lapped the ute's wheels. "We'd better be off. We can make it home for Christmas dinner."

Happiness

There was a packet of sugar somewhere in the cluttered pantry. Sighing, Iouella scrimmaged amongst jars, cans, packets and bits of crockery. With two small children, there just wasn't time to tidy cupboards.

Behind a half-eaten packet of biscuits, she came across an old egg cup. It was white with rabbits dressed in blue painted on its sides. It was cracked and one of the rabbit's ears was faded away, but Iouella couldn't bear to part with it.

Continuing to rummage, she thought about Aunt Bessie who had given her the egg cup when she was a little girl. Aunt Bessie had said the egg cup was full of happiness and louella thought it was too small to hold much happiness. Then Aunt Bess said it was magic and, if you ate up all your egg, the happiness just grew and grew and grew. Furthermore, she said that there was always more happiness in the egg cup the next time you used it.

Louella tossed the biscuits into the rubbish bin and wished Aunt Bess were still alive to tell her own children such wondrous stories.

She rummaged some more as she imagined happiness rising from an egg cup. She wondered if it would be bright like fireworks, or like beautiful music or warm sunshine. Perhaps it would be a soft, gentle mist wrapping around you like the arms of a loved one. She liked that thought.

Her eyes lit on the packet of sugar and she triumphantly snatched it from its hiding place. In her haste, she knocked the eggcup from the shelf and watched in disbelief as it shattered at her feet.

"Oh no!" Her shriek was filled with horror. Could there be happiness now that she had destroyed the eggcup?

"I love you Mummy," three year old Zach hugged her legs and looked up at her with a worried face. She swooped him up in her arms. Of course happiness didn't come from eggcups!

The Real Antoinette

Sister Antoinette Pasqual crept into the confession box and closed the heavy wooden door. She stood for a moment in the silent darkness.

"What can I do for you, my child?" She heard the voice of Father O'Dwyer.

'Father, I have sinned."

"Yes?"

"I love the Holy Father, I love Jesus and the Blessed Virgin Mary but there is a feeling of unrest in my heart. As one who has answered the call to be a Bride of Christ, I shouldn't have such unrest."

"Go on."

"I cannot explain more, Father, but I believe I should be at ease and content in doing the work of the Lord."

"My child, you must pray more sincerely and more often and ask for God's help to overcome this failing. You must do this six times each day as well as saying the rosary at those times. Go now and sin no more."

"Thank you, Father." Sister Antoinette stepped into the dim light of the ancient church. She hadn't told Father O'Dwyer that, for weeks, she had been praying to God about her feelings of unrest far more than six times a day. Sometimes, she was so distracted by her silent prayers that Mother Superior would sigh in exasperation and say, "Sister Antoinette, I don't believe you have heard a word I have said! You really must learn to pay more attention."

Sister Antoinette had almost completed her novice training but, instead of feeling more confident, she doubted herself more each day. Lately, quite disturbing thoughts had come, unbidden, to her mind. She wondered if she was going crazy and if she should have mentioned this in confession. Maybe madness wasn't a sin but some people would surely see it as a weakness.

She made her way to the big kitchen where it was her responsibility to prepare vegetables for that evening's meal. "You're late!" said Sister Martha, "You will need to work fast now."

Sister Eugene, who was young and kind, said, "Don't worry. I will help you."

Sister Antoinette wished she were more like Sister Eugene who always had a smile and was quick to help others. Furthermore, she possessed a sweet voice that never sang out of tune. Sister Antoinette's singing voice seemed to have a will of its own, causing the senior sisters to frown and the younger ones to stifle a giggle.

Peeling one potato after another, Sister Antoinette had an odd feeling that a stranger inhabited her body. It was as if her real self had quietly slipped away somewhere and someone else had taken its place. She didn't know how or when this had occurred.

She picked up a carrot and began to scrape the skin off it. She saw that the carrot was covered in blood then realized she had peeled her finger. She fainted.

Mother Superior was not happy or sympathetic even though Sister Antoinette's finger had required several stitches. The Doctor told her she must not get her finger wet and she must not bump or knock it against anything. She was not able to do many chores so she was told to go to the orphanage to teach the younger children how to read.

Sister Antoinette prayed even more but her unease grew greater still. Somehow, she felt that beyond this life there was a place where her real self existed. She must search for that place.

To reach the orphanage, she had to cross a very large area of park land. The sun shone brightly and ducks swam on a little lake. Sister Antoinette caught sight of a squirrel but she saw no other person. Birds sang in the trees. Hearing this, she felt like singing as well. She barely remembered the songs from her childhood, so she sang something more familiar.

With only the birds and the ducks to hear, her voice rose loud and clear. "Our Father which art in heaven..." her voice soared above the tree tops.

"Hallowed be Thy name..." Every note was pure, unrestrained and joyful.

"Lead us not into temptation..." It seemed that her feet barely touched the path as she walked. Her voice rose higher and she knew God was listening.

"Amen." Sister Antoinette had almost reached the other side of the park land as she sang the last note. She felt warm tears on her cheeks but didn't mind. It was just her eyes overflowing with happiness. She had discovered the place where her real self existed. Tomorrow she would inform Mother Superior she would be leaving the convent to pursue her true vocation, singing.

Station Pier

Marion sighed as she brushed a strand of silver grey hair from her face. It would be her birthday in a few days and it was time to sort out her belongings. She had no intention of dying just yet but, when the time came, she wouldn't have a say in the matter.

Her favourite niece, Rose would be her sole benefactor and Marion didn't want to burden the poor girl with disposing of things that were of no use to her. Additionally, she didn't like the idea of other people rummaging around and laughing at things Marion had held dear. I don't know why I am worrying. After all, I will be dead.

She took nightdresses and pyjamas from a drawer, putting the oldest ones in a plastic bag ready to take to an op shop. From the bottom of the drawer, she took a bundle of papers tied up with pink ribbon. They were letters on tissue thin airline paper. She sat on the tapestry covered chair next to her bed, untied the ribbon and began to read the letters.

We were so young and so much in love! Marion smiled at the foolishness of youth. He had said she was his dream girl. She had believed him. Then came his big news. He had found a job on a luxury cruise ship; he would see the world and make a fortune. When he returned, they would marry. She cried. He said time would fly and he would write.

It was Spring when she stood on Station Pier waving until the big cruise ship was a dot on the horizon. The pier and nearby busy wharves were bathed in warm sunlight; a gentle breeze rippled the blue ocean. Children ate ice cream and families shared fish and chips with sea gulls. Marion was blind to everything but the disappearing ship and the ache in her heart.

Jack kept his promise to write. Airmail letters came from New Zealand, Fiji, America, Panama, Mexico and other places with names that Marion had never before heard. Sometimes he sent post cards and, always, messages of love.

Then, without warning, the letters and post cards stopped coming. Now she smiled as she remembered checking her mail box again and again, as if that would somehow make a letter magically appear. She wrote to him care of the cruiser ship's head office. There was no reply. She phoned his mother who didn't seem to want to speak to her.

Maybe Jack had something to do with her never marrying, not that she had ever linked the two together. She had known some wonderful lovers over the years but she preferred not to commit herself to any man. She enjoyed her freedom and travelled extensively. For some reason beyond her understanding, she had taken the bundle of letters on all of her journeys. She had met many interesting and handsome men in Paris, Rome, Vienna and countless other places. She had never run into Jack. Not that I was looking for him.

There were tears in Marion's eyes as she read the last letter. At my age, I can be forgiven for being sentimental. She tied the pink ribbon around the letters and placed them in her big brown shopping bag.

There was a chill in the air the next day. Marion donned her grey overcoat which was too big for her frail frame. She took her purse and her shopping bag and made her way to Station Pier.

At the pier, she took the ribbon from the letters then

took a letter, dropped it into the water and watched as it disintegrated and sank. She did the same with each letter until they were all gone.

Not far off, a man stood watching her. He adjusted the cap on his balding head, leaving grey hair poking out at the sides. He smoothed his jumper over his ample waist.

The last letter disintegrated and merged with the water. Marion looked up and turned to leave. She saw the man, his familiar face lined and weathered with age.

"It's rather chilly out here. I know a cafe where we can get warm food and drinks."

"It's been a long time, Jack." Marion walked to his side and they strolled towards the cafe.

Jack

Raking up leaves in the front garden was pointless. More dropped from the trees as Benita raked. Her movements slow and robot like, she handled the rake as if it weighed a ton.

Everything was pointless now. She had searched for a meaning and found a gaping wound in her soul, a dark hole threatening to swallow her. At times she longed to be swallowed, to let the darkness block out all thoughts and pain. Keeping busy was the only thing preventing her from surrendering to the darkness.

Across the street, someone was filming her from a white van. At six o'clock, people all over the country would gaze at her image on television screens. She was tired of reporters thrusting microphones towards her and asking, "Mrs Drake, have you heard any more about your little boy?"

"Mrs Drake, how are you feeling?"

"How are you and Mr Drake coping?"

She could find no answers so remained silent.

Inside the house, her husband, Raymond, was also silent. He hadn't spoken since the search was called off three days ago. He sat at the kitchen table, unwashed and unshaven, staring into space. They were both prisoners of grief, incapable of comforting each other. An icy barrier separated them.

Benita knew Raymond's silence was her punishment. He blamed her for what had happened, but no more than she blamed herself. Just the same, she wished he could at least say, "It could happen to anyone." The only person who had said that was a policewoman with tears in her eyes.

Benita knew everyone else blamed her as well. It was a mother's duty to protect her child so it was clearly her fault.

It had happened quickly, in the few moments it took her to let go of Jack's hand and stoop down to pick up his dropped teddy bear. One moment he was there, then he was gone. She searched for him amongst the shoppers and called his name over and over but he was gone.

After that, nothing seemed real and life lost its meaning. Before he became silent, Raymond repeatedly asked, "How could you have let it happen? How could you let go of his hand?"

A policeman had said, "A three year old can be difficult at times. Anyone would understand if you were angry with him."

"I have never been angry with my son," she replied. His eyes said he didn't believe her.

More leaves floated to the grass at her feet. Mechanically, she raked them towards the pile near the roses. As she watched, the leaves turned to pearly sea shells scattered on a sandy beach. Her lips tasted salt and she heard soft lapping of waves on a shore. She used the rake to pile the shells in a shiny heap and then raked the sand, leaving long, shallow furrows.

The cry of a sea gull swooping towards her startled her. She looked up.

A man held a microphone near her face. Another stood nearby with a camera. "Mrs Drake, how do you feel now that he police are no longer searching for your son?" She dropped the rake and went into the house.

Raymond didn't stir as she took her handbag and house keys from the kitchen bench. "I am going to fetch Jack," she said. He didn't reply.

She could have taken the car but her driving had become erratic. She would take a bus to the city, a tram to the waterfront then a ferry across the bay.

At the tram stop in the city, someone tapped her shoulder. An old woman wearing a long floral dress, held out a bony hand. "Could you spare a coin, Love?" Blue eyes peered from a wrinkled face.

Benita placed two gold coins in the outstretched hand. "Thank you," the old woman said, "You are doing the right thing. Intuition is the treasure of a woman's soul." Her skirt dragged on the street as she walked away.

The ferry reached the other side of the bay. Benita stepped off and walked from the pier to the sandy shore. There were many people on the beach.

Benita's path led her around a bend and past high dunes. A small child sat at the water's edge building a sand castle. She walked closer, marvelling at his beauty. Though pale and thinner, his tear stained cheeks were still plump. Brown hair tumbled across his forehead; long lashes partly hid dark eyes as he looked down at his work. His small hands smoothed a pile of sand.

A thin, tired looking, jean clad woman sat nearby. Water lapped at her bare feet.

The boy looked up as Benita's shadow fell over him. "Mummy!" The sand castle was trampled as he ran towards her.

"Jack! My baby!" She clasped him to her, kissing him again and again.

Rising, the other woman took a few steps towards them.

"I have treated him well but I cannot make him happy. He belongs to you."

"Yes. He is my child." The two women gazed at each other, their eyes filled with joy and sadness, understanding and compassion.

"We go home, Mummy?" The boy snuggled against his mother's breast.

"We will go home, Jack." She walked towards the ferry. The other woman walked across the sand in the opposite direction. Neither one looked back.

The Valley of Vilna

Voya was woken by the sound of her stepmother whispering. Carefully, she turned over in her narrow bed at the back of the kitchen and looked towards the fireplace. In the glow of the dying embers, her father and stepmother sat on wooden stools.

Her stepmother touched her husband on the knee. "You know it's for the best, Alexi. Farmer Ilyia Ilyavic will pay us handsomely for Voya and we will never have to worry about being hungry in our old age."

"I'm not sure if it's the right thing, Olga," came her father's whispered reply.

"Alexi, you worry too much. We must act before Voya runs off with some young man who will have nothing to give to her or to us. Ilyia Ilyiavic has sufficient money to pay us and to provide for Voya."

"You think of everything, Olga. I will visit Ilyia tomorrow."

Voya felt as though a stake had been driven through her heart. She was just fifteen years old. She didn't want to marry Ilyia Ilyavic who was almost as old as her father.

The next morning, while her father and stepmother slept, Voya crept from the cottage, taking with her the blanket from her bed, a flask of water, some bread and some cheese. She would go to her grandmother who lived on the other side of the Valley of Vilna. She could travel through the valley, which would take two or three days, or take many more days, passing through several villages and avoiding the valley. She feared that, if she were seen in one of the villages, she would be returned home and forced to marry Ilyia Ilyiavic.

She was afraid of what the Valley of Vilna held but felt she had no choice but to pass through it. It had been many years since anyone dared to enter the valley. Stories were told of neighbours, or cousins, or someone they once knew who had stepped into the valley and never been seen again. Then there were stories about men who had returned from the valley all bloodied and bruised and barely alive.

Those who had returned from the dark forests of the Valley of Vilna had whispered stories about Nilbog, a man with mystical, evil powers. Some said he was a beast, not a man. Others said he was half beast, half man. They all said he had three faces.

Voya would rather face Nilbog than marry Ilyia so she entered the valley. Though she was filled with fear, Voya smiled at the thought of her stepmother waking to a cold cottage and shouting out, "You lazy slattern, why haven't you lit a fire?"

All that day, she trudged through the forest, meeting only birds and other small forest creatures. Many times, she was startled by the sound of a falling twig, the rustle of leaves under her feet or the sighing of the tall trees. She felt a bit better after reasoning that something with three faces must surely be of great size. She would hear it coming from a distance and would have time to make her escape.

As night fell, her fears returned. Fallen logs and thick vines had caused her to travel slowly. She could not see well enough to go any further and would have to spend the night in the forest. Fumbling in the growing darkness, she ate some bread and cheese and drank some water before wrapping herself in the blanket and lying down next to a log.

Afraid to close her eyes, she tried to remember if Nilbog

hunted his victims at night. She had heard so many different stories, it was hard to remember the details. Some said Nilbog had three heads; others said his faces were all on one head. Some said his eyes were all the same colour while others said each pair of eyes was a different colour to the rest. Voya couldn't remember what colour any of the eyes were supposed to be.

In spite of her fear, she fell asleep. She was woken by a mournful, haunting sound. "Mopoke, mopoke, mopoke," it seemed to be saying. The noise echoed through the dark forest.

Terrified, she lay perfectly still for a while, then, opening her eyes, looked up. High in the forest above her, were six enormous white eyes. The sound of "Mopoke, mopoke, mopoke" seemed to come from the eyes. As her own eyes become accustomed to the dark, she saw that the eyes belonged to owls like the ones her grandmother had once shown her in a picture book. Her grandmother had told her that the owls of the Valley of Vilna were unique in that they went in threes instead of pairs.

"Hello Nilbog," she said. Then it was the sound of her laughter that echoed through the forest, drowning out the sound of wings as the owls flew away. She remembered how people who had escaped unharmed from the Valley of Vilda were thought to be sacred and no one dared to question them or deny their wishes. She wouldn't be forced to marry Ilyia now but she would prefer to live with her grandmother. She wrapped the blanket tighter around her body and slept again.

The Corner of James and Henry Street

The still air was heavy with oppression. In alleyways, the smell of rotting garbage hung like fetid mist. For days, dark clouds had been gathering overhead. Yesterday afternoon, thunder rolled across the heavens and echoed between the skyscrapers. Jagged lightning flashes had startled workers in glass towers, sending them scuttling to the centre of the open office spaces. Huge drops of rain fell on the dusty city but stopped before people in the streets had opened umbrellas or darted under awnings.

Air conditioned stores and cafes were crowded. In stores, a few purchased goods they didn't need and could ill afford. Most wandered aimlessly, rifling through stuff on bargain tables or looking at the price on crystal vases they never intended to buy. In cafes, people sat for hours sipping mineral water or iced coffee while they thumbed yesterday's newspapers or last year's magazines.

Sweat trickled down Nick's face and back and behind his knees. His tee shirt clung to his body, the waist band of his shorts was saturated and his sneaker clad feet felt as though they were in ovens. He stood on the corner of James and Henry Street wondering if he should take a tram to the beach and paddle in the cool water. It might be easier to spend an hour or two sipping iced drinks in a cafe. Anything would be better than returning to the stifling boarding house.

He caught the smell of perspiration mixed with cigarettes and heady perfumes as people with drooping shoulders and robotic steps passed him. Constant traffic left exhaust fumes hanging in the air.

The pedestrian crossing lights changed to green, as if prompted by a clap of thunder that rolled overhead, reverberating in the alleys. Like spider veins on the bulbous nose of an alcoholic, a series of lightning flashes lit up the inky clouds. The drooping pedestrians hurried over the crossing, eager to reach shelter.

Nick moved close to the window of a chocolate shop. It shook as more thunder boomed in his ears. Lightning lit the sky again in a dozen places. Then hail thrashed the city and all those who had not found shelter.

The last of the pedestrians reached Nick's side of the street. They shook sodden umbrellas, patted wet hair and brushed at dripping clothes. Some women looked down, to assess the damage to their flimsy high heeled shoes. Each paused for a moment before darting through doorways or racing off close to the walls of buildings in futile attempts to shelter from the hail stones.

A man stopped near Nick, removed dark glasses from his face, wiped them on his sodden green shirt before replacing them. He brushed at his tight legged black pants and stomped water from his pointed fake crocodile skin shoes.

Hail gave way to heavy rain. Muddy water filled the gutters, food wrappers and other city debris swept along in its current.

A heavy set man emerged from the doorway of the chocolate shop. He wore tailored grey pants and a light blue shirt which strained over his paunch. Without a word of greeting, he nodded towards the man with the pointed shoes.

The two men looked at Nick before moving to the shop window on the opposite side of the doorway. Standing close together, they spoke in low tones. Nick was focussed on the sky and the rain and hoping there would be relief from the suffocating heat. He was only vaguely aware of the two men. To him, it seemed the argument began without warning, though, in fact, it might have started a month or years ago.

The men hissed at each other, growing louder by the second. Tailored Pants hissed, "That's not what we agreed!"

Pointed Shoes spoke out loud, emphasising every word. "You can take it or leave it!"

Tailored Pants yelled, "I won't be satisfied until you honour the agreement."

Pointed Shoes turned as if to leave. Tailored Pants stopped him with a blow to the solar plexus followed by a punch to the head which sent the dark glasses flying. Pointed Shoes reeled, stumbled, slipped and fell. His body sprawled on the pavement. His head lay in the gutter.

Tailored Pants looked at Nick who had no intention of staying to chat. Turning left, he fled along James Street until he reached the Botanical Gardens. Panting, he sat on a wooden bench and watched as water ran down his legs into his sneakers.

On the corner of James and Henry Street, rain washed over the body of a man wearing a green shirt, tight black pants and pointed fake crocodile skin shoes. Blood from his mouth and the back of his head turned pink then disappeared as it mingled with the gushing water in the gutter. Sirens wailed in the distance. The man in the tailored grey pants was nowhere to be seen.

The Five Fifteen from Flinders Street

The five fifteen train from Flinders Street was on schedule for a change. I was among the jostling workers and shoppers who crammed into the crowded carriages. Wedged between bodies smelling of sweat, deodorant and perfume, I wished I had taken an earlier train or waited until peak hour was over.

Fearing being trampled to death if I fell, I clung to the back of a seat as the train lurched and jolted. At each stop, the doors opened to suck in more people. I began to think I would suffocate. Adding to my discomfort, a cacophony of mobile phone rings tones and loud, one sided conversations assaulted my ears. Many of the conversations were spoken in a foreign language. Worse still, were the conversations in English describing mundane and even gross personal details.

At the first stop beyond the city proper, the train disgorged a swarm of passengers and mobile phones. Thankfully, they were replaced by a far smaller swarm. After a few more stops, I sighed with relief as I settled into an empty seat.

At each successive stop, the train shed more passengers and collected less. At Box Hill, passengers hurried out of the carriage as if they were late for their own wedding or funeral. There were no more ring tones or shouted conversations. The noise of the train seemed eerily quiet. For a moment, I thought I was on my own but, looking around, I counted five other people scattered throughout the carriage. Like me, they all sat alone. I leaned my head against the window and closed my eyes, thinking to have a little nap before reaching my destination at the end of the line.

Someone stumbling against my legs woke me. "Sorry! Sorry! I don't like sitting by myself at this time of day." She was old and wore her grey hair in plaits coiled around her head. Her clothes were all black and there was a ladder in her panty hose. She spoke with an Italian accent.

I hadn't the heart to be angry with her. "That's all right," I said.

She said she had been to Footscray to visit her daughter who had just had a new baby, the fifth. "My daughter, she has plenty work. Plenty. Too much. I help her a little bit. Wash the clothes and cook something. For the children, you know." The new baby was a boy, the first son and everyone was very happy. I nodded and smiled in what I hoped were all the right places.

From somewhere at the back of the carriage, a tired looking young woman, wearing a red dress tightly stretched over her pregnant abdomen, waddled towards the old woman. She plonked herself on the seat. "Gee, I wish I had someone like you to come and help me. I've got two at school and my husband usually works long hours. My parents are up the country."

Soon, the two women were engaged in a lively conversation about pregnancy, birth and child rearing. The old woman often said, "Where I come from, near Venice, that's how it was always done."

They were exchanging recipe ideas when a handsome young fellow in a business suit sat on the seat next to me. "I hope you don't mind me joining you. I heard talk about Venice. My fiancé and I are getting married next year and we are planning to go there for our honeymoon." His name was Ed.

I was drawn into the conversation as the old woman, who said her name was Concetta, took us for a tour of the streets and lanes, the canals and plazas of Venice.

We drooled at the description of the food to be eaten and "Oohed" over the fine jewellery, clothing and glass ware to be found in the shops.

The pregnant woman said she had never been out of the state except for a trip to Sydney. Her name was Jessica. She thought maybe they could save up for a holiday once they had paid off the house. She rubbed her belly. "The baby's kicking an awful lot lately." Everyone laughed.

An old fellow with a walking stick slowly moved a few seats and settled himself across the aisle. "I've never been to Italy but I've been to New Zealand and I've seen most of Australia in me younger days."

Everyone's attention shifted to the old chap. "So you've travelled a fair bit in Australia?" Ed leaned towards him.

"Yes. Worked all over the place. Mustering, fencing, droving. Could turn me hand to most things. Got the name "Speedy" because I used to be quick on me feet. A bit different now." He tapped his walking stick on the floor.

We listened to tales of flood and relentless drought, of droving cattle across the Kimberleys and driving a heavily laden mail truck along the rutted, sandy Oodnadatta Track. He had fallen in love with a girl in Wagga Wagga. He visited her as often as possible, eventually persuading her to marry him and join his nomadic lifestyle. After their third child, they bought a little house in Bourke, though he was often away for months at a time.

His Nancy was in heaven now and he lived with one of his sons. "I'm not so good at living in the city," he said. "It's kind of lonely and I can't get around so well now. Been thinking about learning computers though I'm probably too old for that sort of thing."

I had barely noticed a young fellow move into the seat opposite Speedy. He wasn't wearing thick glasses but he still looked nerdy. "I'd be happy to teach you about computers and you could tell me more about your travels," he said. His brother had Myalgic Encephalomylitis and he planned to one day ride a bike around Australia to raise money and awareness.

"What's Myalgic Encephalomylitis?" everyone asked, stumbling on the words.

The nerd, who said his name was Freddy, launched into a lengthy explanation of symptoms and statistics of this illness which robbed so many of a normal life and killed others. No one was bored because Freddy was both earnest and funny in his telling. His good humour soon had everyone laughing and swapping more stories about Italy and cooking, pregnancy and kids, weddings and honeymoons, dust and flies on outback tracks, sickness and bike riding. It was all interspersed with snippets of computer technology and what could be found on the net.

I shared bits of my own life and my work with mental illness but it seemed insignificant compared to what I had heard. As we all left the carriage at the end of the line and said our farewells, I decided that I should ride the five fifteen from Flinders Street more often.

Runny Eggs

Jeremiah felt a pang of guilt as he placed two slices of hot, lightly toasted bread on the plate in front of him. There may not be enough bread left for the long line of hungry people waiting for an empty seat. Perhaps it would be gone before even half of them got to sit down. He cast these thought from his mind. It wasn't his fault that others had arrived after him.

His shirt sleeve brushing a bowl of porridge, he reached for the butter. Avoiding the crumbs, honey and jam stuck in it, he helped himself to two generous slabs of butter and watched it slowly melt into the toast. He silently thanked the Parish of St Thomas for this annual St Patrick's Day breakfast. He added another little prayer, asking the good Lord to help him get back on his feet soon. He was tired of sleeping on park benches and winter was on its way. He wasn't a religious person but maybe this great breakfast was a sign that God was looking upon him with a degree of benevolence.

A sharp poke in his left rib cage interrupted his prayers. "Can yer pass the sugar?" The bloke sitting next to Jeremiah looked impatient, his mouth hanging open to reveal a few yellowed teeth.

"Yeah, sure." Jeremiah passed the sugar and resisted the urge to say there was no need to be rude. He wanted to preserve the feeling of contentment as long as possible.

Butter smeared his hands as he cut the toast into fingers and placed them next to two boiled eggs in chipped white egg cups on the middle of his plate. A furtive glance around the table showed that everyone else was absorbed in stirring porridge, helping themselves to jam or cramming food into their mouth. Jeremiah licked his fingers and the knife, taking care not to cut his tongue.

His Grandmother used to slice hot, buttery toast into fingers just like this. She called them "soldiers." He called them "butter fingers" because they made his fingers all buttery. Grandmother would scold when he licked his fingers but he knew she was never really cross with him. She would probably never have imagined that he would one day dine at a place like this.

He sliced the top off the eggs with swift movements and watched yellow yolk slide down the sides. Clear albumin was mixed with the yolk. The eggs were undercooked. Grandmother always cooked them just right. He sprinkled salt and pepper from jam smeared shakers.

His Grandmother's salt and pepper shakers were white with blue windmills patterned on the side. They sat permanently beside a matching sugar bowl on the kitchen table. Jeremiah wondered what had become of all the little things Grandmother had treasured. He'd once heard a rumour that her house had been sold to pay her debt. He couldn't imagine how she had grown so poor. There had always been enough money to buy the essentials and an occasional treat, though he sometimes waited a while for expensive things like new shoes.

Grandmother filled his thoughts a lot lately. As the toast, warm and soggy with butter and egg, slid down his throat, he remembered her warm, squashy hugs. "Why don't I have a mother like everyone else?" he would ask. He never asked about his father.

Grandmother would answer, "Don't worry. She will come to her senses one day and come back."

He used to believe her. Then it was he who came to his senses, realizing his mother was never coming back.

After Vietnam, he lost his senses again, wandering aimlessly in a psychedelic haze. He emerged long enough to learn that Grandmother had gone to her Maker. He slipped back into the haze and stayed there until he woke to find himself an unwilling guest of a Mental Asylum.

Jeremiah soaked up the last of the runny egg with the last bit of toast and swallowed it. He collected his crockery and cutlery and put them on a trolley standing at the side of the room. An old man quickly limped to the vacant seat and was served by volunteers. Jeremiah filled a disposable cup with coffee from an urn. Outside, he joined a group of others leaning against a wall as they drank coffee, smoked cigarettes and exchanged inane conversation.

"Good feed, hey?"

"My oath!" They rubbed skinny bellies and wiped their mouths with the back of a hand. Some laughed and cursed people visible only to them.

Jeremiah wondered if a psychedelic haze might not be such a bad thing, but he began walking towards where Grandmother used to live. His belly was warm and full, the taste and smell of breakfast lingering in his mouth and nostrils. Weaving in and out of the crowds, his mind couldn't remember which way to go, but his feet remembered.

He expected to find an ugly apartment block on the sight but he could see no tall building rising above others. He wondered if his feet had taken him the wrong way after all.

He drew nearer and knew it was the right spot. Grandmother's house stood there, sparkling with a new coat of white paint. An old woman wearing a purple coat and matching hat was letting herself in the front door. As if sensing his presence, she turned and looked at Jeremiah. Her face was long and thin, not round like Grandmother's.

“Who are you?” she asked.

“Jeremiah. I used to live here.”

“I came back but you had left. Welcome home son.” She ran towards him with outstretched arms.

The Sacred Mat

Their faces creased with worry, the tribal elders sat in a circle on the sacred mat. They spoke in anxious tones and sometimes uttered loud wails. They were trying to find a solution to a problem far greater than anything they had ever known.

Kartjellakoo sat a little distance away making spears from strong slender sticks. The tribal elders had taught him how to do this when he was a young boy. They had taught him many other things. He had learned well and the elders had been pleased with him but he held a secret which he had never shared with them. A secret that plagued his days and haunted his nights. He was sure he was the cause of the great problem they were trying to solve.

The sacred mat was made from feathers of every bird in the land, woven together with strips of kangaroo skin and hairs from the long beards of elders. The weaving formed an intricate pattern of circles and whirls, capturing the spirits of the birds and kangaroo and the wisdom of the elders. The nature of the weaving was a skill passed by elders from one generation to the next.

Each time the elders met, they sat on the sacred mat. After every three summers, the mat was washed in clear, running water to remove any evil spirits which had crept into it. After every twelve summers, a new mat was woven and the old one was burned, releasing its spirits to the dream time. A great corroboree was held to farewell the old and welcome the new. If these rituals were not kept, the Rainbow Serpent would become very angry.

Kartjellakoo's hands trembled as he worked and listened to the elders. It was time to wash the sacred mat but there had been very little rain for the past five summers. The streams and rivers had shrunk, their waters brown and sluggish. Once gushing waterfalls had dried up or were reduced to a trickle too small to wash the sacred mat. Food was hard to find. One old man and two children had died from starvation.

Kartjellakoo remembered a day five summers ago when he angered the Rainbow Serpent. The young girl's body and limbs were smooth and shiny like the stones he sometimes fashioned into axes. He had gone to fish in a lagoon not far from the camp. She was standing amongst the water lilies. When she smiled at him, he experienced a feeling that was both wonderful and terrifying.

Wading towards her, he noticed her small, firm breasts. His voice turned to a croak as he asked "Who are you? Why are you here?"

She told him her name was Milba and she was from a neighbouring tribe. She was gathering water lily stems for food and reeds to make baskets.

He knew it was forbidden to take a woman from another tribe without permission from the elders but he didn't care. Milba's soft body yielded to his as they lay among the reeds by the lagoon. Now, the lagoon had almost disappeared and there were no longer water lilies.

The elders decided that, if the rain didn't come after two moons, the tribe would perform a rain dance. Kartjellakoo was still listening. If the rain dance doesn't work, I will tell the elders my secret. They will put a curse on me and I will die slowly and painfully but the Rainbow Serpent will stop being angry. Rain will come, the sacred mat will be washed and my people will have food.

The men chanted as their feet stamped a rhythmic beat

on the dusty earth. Their black bodies were decorated with white ashes and ochre; feathers adorned their heads and ankles. As they circled the camp fire, their chants grew louder, competing with the monotonous sound of a didgeridoo. Above, the moon and stars were suspended from a cloudless sky.

Two moons passed. Kartjellakoo lay sleepless by the camp fire while the rest of the tribe slept in a cave. Tomorrow, he would ask to meet with the elders.

He was startled by loud thunder. Soon, he felt the rain on his body, he tasted it and he smelt it. He danced for joy.

The rain continues almost without break for three days; long enough to saturate the earth, to fill the lagoons and to cause the rivers and waterfalls to flow. It was time to wash the sacred mat.

Not many moons after, Kartjellakoo was called to a meeting with the elders. Afraid, his eyes were downcast as he sat on the sacred mat. Wiradhuri, the oldest of them all, said, "Kartjellakoo, you are now a man. We have chosen a woman for you. She is from another tribe and her name is Milba." He knew then that the Rainbow Serpent had forgiven him.

The Sleeping Giant

He groaned as he slept. A low, sighing kind of groan. He lay on one side and drool escaped from a corner of his mouth onto dry soil beneath his head. A black beetle ran across his face, its legs catching in the greying stubble. It paused near the drool then ran down his chin on to his neck, across his shoulder, his arm and to the ground. Groaning again, he made a slight shift in his lower body.

He was a big man. A giant of a man. His crop of grey streaked black hair hadn't been cut for a while. The skin on his face and on his arms below his short sleeved red shirt was tanned and leathery. He looked like an outdoor man. His hands were large and calloused and dirt lay beneath his fingernails. His long legs were clad in dark dungarees, his feet in large scuffed black boots.

Dougal McLean rolled onto his other side, causing drool to trickle back over his face. A fresh lot gradually found its way out the other side of his mouth. Still asleep, he snorted and licked at the drool.

He became aware of something digging into the flesh of his left thigh. His hand found a small flattened orange juice carton, the kind that kids drink from through a straw. The kind that has information, mostly in small print, on it. Information to say that the contents are mainly water and sugar and preservatives and other stuff and only a little bit of real orange juice. The straw was missing.

Awake now, Dougal was dazed and unsure of his where-abouts, though he had discovered he was lying next to a wire mesh fence. He sat up, propping himself against the fence. He felt hot and thirsty. There was a queer light around him; a yellowish glow. Something strange was happening.

Slowly, he began to remember, bits of information dropping into his head like water though a leaking roof. Drip, drip, drip. He recognised the local sports ground and remembered that he had been watching a charity cricket match. He couldn't remember which side was winning. There had been a sausage sizzle, cup-cakes, raffles, coffee and beer. All for a good cause. He must have had one of his blackouts. That had been happening a lot lately. A couple of months ago, a Doctor had said he should have more investigations but he'd put it off. His alpacas needed tending, there were fences to mend and he needed to do something about the water pump before he had to rely on the muddy creek water.

He didn't know how long he had lain unconscious against the fence. His watch said it was 5pm. Something was stinging his eyes and perspiration ran from his forehead. There was an eerie quietness around him. No bird sounds. No human voices.

He looked around. The place was deserted. "Where have all the people gone?" he asked the darkened emptiness.

His body felt like a big jelly baby, unresponsive to his commands. Somehow, he managed to stand up, planting his wide apart feet firmly on the ground. Something touched his cheek. He wiped at it with the middle finger of his left hand, at the same time as he became aware of an acrid smell. He looked at his finger. Black soot. More began to fall about and on him.

He looked up towards the East, where there ought to have been hills. All he could see was smoke and leaping flames moving towards the valley below, where his house and his alpacas were. Now he could hear a roar and crackling. Soot and embers rained down on him, blackening him and catching in his eyelashes. His truck was where he had left it and stood alone in the car park. His body was both leaden and jelly like but, somehow, he ran.

The next morning, the fire fighters came. They found the charred remains of his house, sheds and his truck. His olive grove and grape vines were destroyed. His property was just a blackened ruin. Fire fighters wiped tears from their tired, grimy faces as they searched the ruins. Their voices were tremulous as they shouted, "Dougal, big man, where are you mate?"

Eventually, the blue heeler dog, its coat muddy, its tongue lolling out, found the fire fighters. It led them to the edge of the creek where a giant of a man lay sleeping, alpaca. Forty or more alpacas lay scattered around him in exhausted clumps. They were all breathing.

Geerrummp

Jasmine had been serving coffee at the Simply Sumptuous Café for sixteen years. Day after day from the time she left school.

"A table for two, Sir?'

"Would you like cream or ice cream with that, Madam?"

"Do take a seat and I will be with you in a moment."

"Would you like to try our blueberry tart?"

She was careful not to spill coffee into saucers. She smiled as she replaced cutlery dropped on the floor. She wiped crumbs from tables and collected crumpled paper napkins which she suspected had been used to wipe noses.

Jasmine longed for something else. She felt there were better, more exciting things waiting somewhere for her. If only she had the courage to look for them.

One day in the middle of summer, the café was very busy and the customers more demanding than usual. Perhaps the heat made them forget to smile or say, "Please" or "Thank you." They were behaving like petulant children.

"My coffee is not hot enough!"

"I asked for two scoops of ice cream, not one!"

"There's no sugar on this table!"

"My apple pie isn't warm!"

Right there, in front of the customers, Jasmine removed her bright red apron, folded it and placed it on the only empty chair. Then she collected her handbag from behind the counter and walked out. Her boss, Deidre McFarlane, said, "Where are you going?" Jasmine didn't reply or turn around. She just walked out.

She went to the river and sat leaning against a big gum tree. Sitting in the shade and listening to the gurgling water was a good feeling. She saw her reflection in the water. Her face looked younger and prettier, less round and more heart shaped. Her hair looked glossy instead of a mousey brown.

She laughed. "Look at that. The water must be magic." She didn't believe in magic but maybe something magic had happened to give her the courage to walk out of the café. She wondered what she should do next.

From somewhere close bye there was a noise like, "Geerrummp, geerrummp." Jasmine scanned the river bank."

"Geerrummp, geerrummp, geerrummp." A frog with a blue back sat on a toad stool at the water's edge. It watched her with yellow green eyes.

"Hello frog."

"Geerrummp."

"I'm pleased to meet you."

"Geerrummp."

"I did something amazing today, frog."

"Geerrummp."

"Do you want to hear what I did? I will tell you anyway."

So Jasmine told the frog what she had done. Then she blew it a kiss. "Thanks for listening."

Suddenly, the frog vanished. "Oh!" said Jasmine, "Don't leave."

"I'm here." A fair haired man in a blue suit stood before her. His eyes were yellow green.

"Where did you come from?"

"From that toad stool over there. Fred Geerrummp at your service."

"Don't be silly! A frog was sitting on that toad stool and frogs don't turn into men."

"In this case, a frog did turn into a man." He told her he was once a gold smith making jewellery for the rich and famous. An unhappy customer, who was secretly a sorcerer, put a curse on him, turning him into a frog. The curse could only be broken if a brave woman blew him a kiss. "Pray tell me your name."

"Jasmine Carruthers. I am not sure that I am brave."

"Well you broke the spell and saved me from a life of eating flies. I am very grateful. Will you come with me to see what has become of my shop?"

They walked hand in hand down the main street. Every few steps, Fred hopped on two feet. "I am afraid I've not practised walking for a while."

Deidre McFarlane was closing the cafe when they passed. "I should have known you were up to some hanky panky." Her lips were pursed.

Jasmine smiled. Fred did another hop.

Warning Signs

As she huddled wedged between a dumpster and a brick wall behind a row of shops, the trembling woman pulled her blood spattered cardigan closer to her body. A cold wind blew drops of rain onto her face. They mingled with blood, turning it pink then trickling down onto her clothes.

Even before darkness fell, she had barely been able to see through her swollen eyes. It was a wonder she had made her way to this spot. She had no particular destination in mind. She had just stumbled along, her only aim to get away from the house. From him.

She coughed then groaned as searing pain gripped her rib cage. She cursed her stupidity. She had seen it coming. Seen the warning signs. As usual, she'd told herself it wouldn't be so bad this time, she would be able to placate him, calm him. She should have learned by now.

At twenty, Libby had fallen madly in love with the handsome young Daniel. Unlike most of the rowdy young men she knew, he was quiet and mysterious, even brooding at times. She was drawn to him like a magnet, craving to know the dark secrets behind the quietness. The foolishness of youth!

Though it was difficult to breathe through her nose, the sour smell of rotting vegetable matter permeated her nostrils. The rain was heavier and Libby wondered if she could crawl beneath the dumpster. Then the pain of breathing reminded her some of her ribs were probably fractured and there was no way she could manoeuvre herself under the dumpster. She needed medical attention but at least she was alive. She had taken nothing when she fled. Not even her handbag or phone.

The charm of Daniel's moodiness and quietness wore off early in the marriage. Ever hopeful, Libby thought he would one day change; she would learn how to handle him. After all, she had taken her wedding vows seriously.

Years passed and the beatings worsened. She sometimes sought refuge somewhere but only long enough for the pain to subside and the bruises to start turning from purple to green. To no avail, people advised, even begged, her to leave. A different kind of magnetism pulled at her. She wanted to outsmart him, to see him get his comeuppance, to see him a broken man. So she always returned.

Lack of energy and difficulty breathing stopped her from screaming in pain as she raised the lid of the dumpster a little way. With one hand, she rummaged through the smelly garbage finding a polystyrene box and a couple of flattened cardboard cartons. Easing herself down, she sat leaning against the brick wall and covered herself with her finds.

She had seen it coming. Daniel's mood had grown steadily more ominous over the last week. He had exploded a few times, slammed doors, flung his meal on the floor and smashed a framed photo of her mother. Each incident had released some of his anger. Not enough. The tension continued to mount. When he lost money on a horse race, she knew this would be the day the volcano blew. She should have left immediately. Well, she wouldn't be returning.

Garbos found her with the polystyrene box over her head and sodden cardboard covering the rest of her body. Police came to the hospital to interview her. She didn't wish to lay charges.

A week later, when she was deemed fit for discharge, a nurse asked her, "Who will be collecting you?"

"Please call my husband," she replied. Next time, she would leave as soon as she saw the warning signs.

A Little Holiday Romance

Esmerelda's usually pale skin was turning a pleasing shade of bronze in the Mediterranean sun. Too soon, she would be returning to Melbourne where the weather was still cool and, more often than not, the sky overcast. She considered staying put right here on the Island of Brac, so close to Croatia that you could almost reach out and touch it.

Shifting her position on the beach chair, she turned a page of the book she wasn't really reading. She spoke a few words of the language but would need to learn it properly. She would miss her friends and she would need to find something more useful than being a tourist to occupy her time. She told herself she was a silly old fool to think of turning her life upside down for a stranger. Just the same, she looked forward to dinner with him that evening.

They dined outdoors where they watched the tide slowly slipping from the shore and the evening fade to night. Wearing cream slacks and an open neck blue shirt, Svak looked younger than his age. Esmerelda's simple white cotton dress showed off her sun tan. The stroganoff was tasty and filling though she wasn't quite used to so much salt in her food. The chilled wine was mellow and fruity. She felt light hearted and young.

"I hope you've enjoyed your stay here in my little hometown of Pucisca," Svak looked at her over the rim of his glass.

"It's a beautiful, beautiful place but there's one thing I will regret not having seen before I leave." There was mischief in her eyes.

"What's that?"

"A vampire."

"There's still time."

Svak still remembered the day, though he was no more than a toddler at the time. The town was smaller then and nearly all of the population had gone to the graveyard. Everyone carried a stick or a shovel or some other weapon. Borne on his father's shoulders, Svak had been scared and bewildered. He could still see the young boy riding the black horse. His father said that the boy and the horse were searching for vampires.

"You've gone very quiet," Esmerelda said.

He smiled. "Just wondering how I can arrange for you to meet a vampire."

They both laughed, then went on to talk about local legends and beliefs. "Of course, no one believes in vampires now," he said. She told him a tale about a Bunyip.

Two men had led the horse and the boy around the grave yard. They came to a very old grave and the horse propped, its nostrils flaring and its eyes rolling in fright. The crowd tore the grave apart with their weapons, unearthing the skeletal remains of a human. They hacked off the legs and drove an iron stake through the ribs, pinning the skeleton to the earth. Then they covered the grave with stones gathered from nearby fields. It had been the grave of his great, great, great grandfather.

Esmerelda talked about Melbourne as they ate very sweet pastry and drank very strong coffee. "I don't think you are really listening, Svak. Are you still thinking about that vampire I am yet to meet?"

His laugh came from somewhere deep in his chest and Esmerelda became aware that was one of the things she liked, maybe loved about him. "I'm not sure how I will arrange that. Did you know that vampires used to be staked through the heart to the ground so they couldn't roam around after they died?"

Esmerelda shivered. "Grisly."

"Well, like I said, it's just a myth,"

He knew it wasn't a myth. He'd had a taste for fresh blood since he was a small boy, though he had never tasted human blood. He had slaked his thirst on the blood of animals. Rabbits, sheep, goats. Even a dog. He was not like some of the things he had heard about vampires. His teeth were sharp but not pointed but he knew what he was.

The wine had left her feeling relaxed and a bit dreamy. The water sparkled with reflections of town lights as they walked bare footed along the sandy beach. They held hands as the path steepened to a cliff top. Stopping, they gazed down at the town and the boats anchored in the little harbour far below.

Once again, she questioned her own sanity but what harm could come from a little holiday romance?

"You are very special," Svak murmured as he stooped to kiss her. She craned her neck to reach his lips.

Tourists found her body below the cliff as the tide came in next day. Someone remarked that it was unusually pale, as though her blood had been drained from her.

Mango Island

For several days, the heat and humidity had intensified, sucking strength from Annabelle and leaving her like a piece of worn out elastic. She gazed at an endless ocean as if to conjure up a sea breeze and white sails on the horizon. Then she looked at the sky, as if, there among the clouds, an aeroplane might suddenly appear.

"I reckon we are in for a big storm. We'd better make sure everything is secure," Emmerson spoke quietly. The concern on his face spoke loudly. He remembered another big storm.

Tattered clothes exposed sweat varnished skin as they sat cleaning that morning's catch of fish. They had done well and would have full bellies that day. Threatening clouds gathered overhead casting a miasma of fear about the man and woman as they worked. They didn't speak about it.

"It's been two years today," Annabelle said as she dropped the cleaned fish into a bucket of water.

"Well, that's something to celebrate!" Emmerson's voice held a hint of sarcasm. Throwing his hands in the air, he did a little jig in the sand and called out, "Did you hear that, all you trees and vines and plants, all you creatures? We've been here two years." His laughter was hollow.

"We had better check the boat moorings," Annabelle turned towards the big yacht anchored in shallow water. She knew it had been two years because she kept a journal. These days, her writing was small and cramped with many abbreviations. She worried what she would do when her note books were all full and her pens were dry. How would she record all that had happened to them? At first, when they thought their stay would be short, they used bits of paper to light fires. Now she regretted burning those tissue boxes and labels from canned food.

Two and a half years ago, they were a little drunk as they celebrated their youngest child moving out. "Now we are free to have a big adventure," Emmerson had said. They drank more wine and talked well into the night, finally deciding to sail around the world. With a few modifications, their yacht, Bessie, would be up to such a journey. "Just think, sunbaking on the deck and no house work," Annabelle drunkenly enthused.

"You won't get off that easy. We will have to take it in turns to be at the tiller." Emmerson laughed.

Six months later, with modified plans and a modified Bessie they set sail from Sydney Harbour on the way to Fiji. Bessie's keel hummed as her hull sliced through blue waters. At times, dolphins swam along beside them. Annabelle remembered the night she handed Emmerson a mug of coffee as he sat at the tiller. It was a bit after midnight. The inky sky was lit by stars as Bessie cut through moon beams on the water. "Good sailing, my love. I will get some sleep and relieve you at six." Annabelle's heart was filled with happiness as she kissed Emmerson's brow.

Emmerson replied." It's so lovely out here I could keep sailing right around the world."

Within two hours, Bessie was tossed around like a piece of driftwood. Beneath her was the ocean gone mad, above her, the heavens had joined the lunacy. Between them, a terrifying fury was unleashed. Rain falling in sheets met with waves higher than Bessie's mast. Forked lightning illuminated the yacht as it floundered like a drowning elephant.

They would have been swept overboard had they stayed on deck so they took refuge in the main cabin. Battered by flying objects and being repeatedly hurled about in the confined space, thoughts of death were never far from their minds.

Annabelle helped Emmerson check the anchors and the ropes attaching the yacht to sturdy trees. She remembered the eerie quietness when she woke in a couple of inches of water on the cabin floor. Emmerson lay almost on top of her, blood drying around a wound on his forehead. She didn't know if they had fallen asleep or been knocked unconscious.

Bessie had lost her mast and there was a hole in the top of the aft cabin. Gone, too, were her rudder and radar. None of the communication devices were working. Somehow, the inflatable dinghy and its motor were unscathed.

Battered and bruised, they drifted for days with no idea where they were. They patched the roof of the aft cabin with sail bags then set about restoring some kind of order on the mast less, rudderless craft. Though they tried to remain hopeful, their hearts were filled with despair as they drifted at the whim of winds and ocean currents. Late one afternoon, they drifted near a small island and, with the help of the dinghy, manoeuvred Bessie close to shore. Somewhere inside them, a quivering kind of hope was born.

They expected to be found soon enough. Folk at home would notify the authorities that contact had been lost. There would be search planes, maybe a Navy ship. Neither plane nor ship came. Annabelle supposed they were presumed drowned, but surely the island was on a map and someone knew of it.

Annabelle coaxed the fire back to life so she could cook the fish before the storm broke. They had used sails to erect a shelter over the fireplace but it wasn't reliable in heavy rain. Wearily, she added coconut milk and pieces of mango to the fish in the blackened pan. Ever since their own supplies had run out, they'd existed on such food. Not far from the shore, was a natural spring so there was plenty of fresh water. Mango and papaya trees grew in abundance but when the fruit was not in season, they relied entirely on sea food. Their diet was far from adequate.

Annabelle watched Emmerson while he tightened the ropes on the shelter. He was a bag of bones, his skin a dry brown parchment. The scar on his forehead had faded but was still visible. His hair, cut short with blunt scissors, stuck up in uneven greying clumps. Her own thin limbs were a reminder that she looked no better. These days, they tired very easily. Without proper food, they couldn't last another year.

She wondered which one of them would die first. Whoever it was, might at least be buried by the other. The last to go would lay where they died.

They had crockery but ate from the blackened pan. Their "adventure" had bound them one to the other in a way nothing else could. Forks dipping in and out of the pan symbolised their unity. Life was hard yet they were content with the company of each other and, in a way, they had grown fond of the place they called Mango Island.

The worst of the storm passed them by. Bessie strained against her moorings and their cooking fire had been dowsed but they suffered no real harm. Emmerson thought it a good omen.

The next day, they went to the spring to bathe and wash clothes. How they longed for some soap and shampoo! They didn't immediately recognise the droning sound overhead. Then, ignoring their nakedness, they ran to the shore, shouting and waving. Sunshine glinted off an aeroplane disappearing into the western sky.

For several weeks, they looked skyward straining their ears to hear that droning noise once again. It never came.

The tide was at its highest when Annabelle and Emmerson stood with water lapping their ankles. They surveyed the place that had been their home for two years. Emmerson called out, "Thank you Mango Island for giving us shelter." Sweat varnished skin glinting in the early morning light, they bowed before turning and walking into the ocean, towards the horizon. Slowly, they walked further and further as water rose higher and higher around their bodies. They were still holding hands when the water rose above their heads. They walked just a little further.

Love

Simon Sinclair, Solicitor, had gotten to know Amelia Medhurst fairly well since setting up practise in Hobart twenty years ago. He met her for the first time soon after the death of her husband, Sterling. She had needed a bit of help to sort out Sterling's estate and to transfer the boarding house business into her name. With her tall, slim figure, unruly auburn hair, high cheekbones and hazel eyes, reddened by sorrow at the time, she was a striking looking woman. However, it was not long before he realised that her strong opinions and her avoidance of most conventions were far more striking than her appearance.

Amelia eschewed feminine frills and flounces in favour of more practical shirts and trousers. Strangely, this had the effect of adding to rather than detracting from her attractiveness. Simon got to know of men who lusted for the widow Medhurst. Amelia was aware of these lustings but she declared that she had no interest in looking for another man. No one could replace Sterling.

During one of their meetings, Simon had asked, "Have you considered what you would like to happen with your estate when you are no longer here?"

"I have considered but haven't made a decision. I have no close family and I won't leave anything to some distant relative I've never met. Maybe when I am older, I will sell everything and go on a cruise. Lots of cruises. Live a life of luxury until I'm in a nursing home and no longer care about anything."

Amelia Medhurst continued to run the boarding house, tend her garden and sell home grown pickled and preserved goods at fetes and markets. She campaigned for various causes, argued with ministers of religion and sometimes fell foul of the local council. Her unruly hair turned to a faded rust colour then to pure white. Her eyesight dimmed and arthritis bent some of her fingers and toes.

It was a sultry day in early December when Simon noticed she had made an appointment with him. "Well, Simon," she said, "It's time to make a will."

He took up a pen to write notes. "I'm glad you've taken my advice at last. Let's start with a list of what you want to bequest and the names of the beneficiaries."

"There's no need to make lists. I'm leaving everything to the Donnybrook Donkey Sanctuary."

"A Donkey Sanctuary?"

"Yes, Hundreds of donkeys die from mistreatment every year."

"It's a big thing to leave everything to donkey sanctuary. Everything! It might be wise to wait until I have made some inquiries."

Amelia wouldn't be dissuaded and the will was made. Simon felt great unease. He wondered if his client was dementing. He was determined to look into this donkey business. Amelia smiled broadly as she left his office. Two hours later, she was back, her jeans and sweater torn.

Simon was about to close the office for the day when came racing in all out of breath. "Good grief! Whatever has happened?"

"I must change the will! Right now!"

In Melbourne, Esmay Croft was surprised to receive a letter from Simon Sinclair, a Solicitor in Hobart. She had attended a conference there seven or eight years ago but knew no one there. She scanned the letter. Who was Amelia Medhurst and why had she left her entire estate to Esmay? It must be a mistake. She called the solicitor the following week.

That night, as Thompson snored, Esmay lay in darkness remembering. After the conference in Hobart, she stayed for a couple of days to explore the place. One afternoon, she wandered into a large park. Admiring the splendid display of plants and flowers, she followed a path past a duck pond. Ahead of her was a grey haired, sprightly woman. The woman bent as if to smell a rose but overbalanced and fell amongst the thorny bushes. Esmay hurried to help the woman to her feet.

"Thank you. How silly of me! I'm not hurt. Can't say the same for my clothes."

Esmay wanted to be sure the woman wasn't injured so insisted they have coffee at a café near the park entrance. The woman's face was lined and drooped with age but there was beauty in her strong features. "Call me Amelia. What's your name?" Esmay may have given her last name. She couldn't remember. She did remember that they chatted easily as if they had known each other for ages.

Esmay was wearing a small silver heart, engraved with the word "Love" on a chain around her neck. Amelia remarked on it. "It was on a bracelet my mother gave me at birth. I can't bear to part with it. Not even to give to my daughter," Esmay didn't mention that she was adopted. Amelia had been friendly and grateful for Esmay's help but why would she will everything to someone she had met only once for a very short time?

The boarding house was empty and falling into disrepair but possibly worth a great deal of money. Simon Sinclair said, "There is something else Amelia wanted you to have." He handed Esmay a brown envelope. Inside was a receipt for a silver baby bracelet with a silver heart, engraved with the word "Loved" attached. The receipt was dated the month Esmay was born.

Somewhere Warm

Amy felt colder than ever before though winter was still in its infancy. She hoped she would find somewhere warm to sleep tonight but there was no point in worrying about it. She had all day.

Right now, she was intent on getting to the Salvation Army store. Cold and dampness from the wet streets had seeped through the holes in the soles of her shoes, making her arthritic toes ache. The Salvos had been good to her. They might give her a pair of shoes for free, especially as it was not pension week. They'd given her the shopping jeep she used to cart around her few possessions. It was better than carrying plastic bags that split open letting things fall out to be lost.

Pausing for a moment, Amy adjusted her woollen beanie and her big black coat, tucking her long gray hair under the collar. Her hair felt greasy and lank. She couldn't remember the last time she had showered and used shampoo.

The wheels of the shopping jeep squeaked and wobbled as she dodged around other pedestrians. Her nostrils and taste buds were teased by the aroma of coffee, raisin toast, sausages, fried eggs, bacon and garlic as she passed cafes and restaurants. Her feet were frozen and the pain in her toes growing worse. "It would be nice to rest for a while in one of those places and have some warm coffee but they wouldn't want someone like me in there," she told herself. She must have spoken out loud because a woman clutching a small child gave Amy a wide berth.

An overflowing rubbish bin seemed to beckon her.

Uncaring, well fed people wearing warm clothes and smelling of soap and shampoo and perfume or aftershave threw away all manner of things. Half eaten sandwiches or hamburgers, half full milk shake containers, apples with barely a bight taken from them. "They would rather throw stuff away than give me a miserable coin."

Sometimes other useful things could be found. Amy had once found a perfectly good glove which she sometimes wore on her left hand.

Now, Amy searched for the treasure amongst the trash but found nothing. Earlier, there was one cold potato chip in another bin. A policeman had chased her from a bin outside McDonalds. "The way he behaved, you'd think he wanted it all for himself."

The pain in her toes was becoming unbearable. Amy leaned heavily on the shopping jeep and walked on her heels, causing an ache in her knees. "I suppose I will have to let them put me in one of those homes. Don't like the thought of that. Rules and regulations. No freedom." She paused to lean against a store window.

After a few minutes, she tugged her beanie down over her ears and her coat collar up to meet it. "Not far to go now. Perhaps they will let me sit and rest for a while at the Salvation Army place. It will be warm in there."

Leaning on the shopping jeep, Amy hobbled away from the store window. Muffled by her beanie and coat collar, she heard a trundling noise coming towards her. Looking up, she saw a boy on a skate board hurtling her way. She tried to move back toward the store window but she was slow and awkward. In an instant, the boy, the skate board, the shopping jeep and Amy all lay on the pavement in a jumbled heap.

The boy stood up and rubbed his knees. Amy lay still and quiet. Blood trickled from her mouth. There was no longer a need to find somewhere warm.

Knock, Knock, Knockin'

Surrounded by mist and cloud, I had no idea where I was or how I had gotten there. I instinctively tried to draw my clothing closer to protect my body from the cool, moist air. With a jolt, I realised I was wearing a flimsy, shapeless white garment, tied at the back. Then my hands discovered I was wearing knickers, sensible knickers with good coverage. That was a comfort of sorts. I wore not another stitch of clothing. No shoes.

My glasses were skew-whiff on my face but they didn't count as clothing. I wiped them on the hem of the white garment and put them back on my face, straight and in line with my eyes. Giant pearly gates loomed up before me. On either side, a giant pearly wall stretched forever. I must be dead, I said to myself. This must be heaven.

The surgeon had said there would be a bit of a risk, but not much. Nothing to worry about. Just a little nick in my throat. Slowly, I reached up with my right hand. The dressing was too big for just a little nick. They must have cut my jugular vein and now I was dead.

I am here now so I might as well go in. There was no handle or latch so I pushed as hard as I could but the pearly gates didn't budge. Looking up, I saw a window in the wall on the left of the gates. A notice said, "Closed for lunch. Back at 1pm." Without a watch I couldn't tell what time it was. What should I do? There were no seats and the clouds didn't look very sturdy. If I stood on one, I could end up floating around in outer space for millions of years. I rested one foot on the other. I had no option but to wait.

My eyes were half closed and I would have fallen asleep

if I hadn't sensed a movement behind the window. Someone was there, with their back to me. Someone dressed in white, someone with long snowy hair. Perhaps there are no hairdressers in Heaven.

At my timid knock, the someone turned to look at me. Half hidden by a long white beard and big bushy eyebrows, was a face more wrinkled than a Pug. Eyes black as ebony peered at me. He slid open the window. Is this heaven? I croaked. The surgeon must have severed my voice along with my jugular.

His voice was like thunder. You're not quite there. You're knock, knock, knockin' on Heaven's door. In this case it's a window.

That's a song, I croaked.

Bob Dylan. What's your name?

I told him and asked if he was Saint Peter.

How did you ever guess? He turned to a computer screen. Somehow I hadn't imagined Heaven being connected to the internet.

He clicked the mouse and scrolled up and down, a frown appearing amongst his Pug like wrinkles. Not here. No. No. Not there either. I wonder... Ah, yes. Here you are. In the No Entry file. Jimnatoon.

That's not my name. You've got the wrong person.

Sometimes we change people's names and yours has been changed to Jimnatoon, filed under No Entry.

That's not me. That's a stupid name. It can't be me.

You're a stupid person so you've been given a stupid name. His black eyes glared at me. No entry.

But I'm not a bad person

You stole lollies from a shop.

I was just a kid.

You pinched your father's cigarettes.

Only two, I swear!

You wagged school.

Not very often.

Saint Peter kept scrolling; kept reminding me of past sins.

I was young and foolish.

You cheated on your husband.

Only once and I was drunk. I'm different now. I've learned my lesson.

You're a drunk.

Being drunk once doesn't make me a drunk.

That's true. He kept scrolling. Hmm. Hmm.

In spite of the moist, chilly air, I broke into a sweat imagining the fires of Hell.

At last, he looked up. There have been no serious misdemeanours for quite some time. Perhaps there is room for leniency.

I am sure I will be a good citizen of Heaven, Saint Peter, Sir.

Not that lenient.

I waited as he stroked his beard with one hand and tugged at his left eyebrow with the other. Yes, yes. That's it. Go back and try again in a couple of years.

How can I do that? I don't know how I got here. I don't

know how to find the road home.

You will work it out. His voice echoed all round me.

I heard someone singing, "Knock, knock, knockin' on Heaven's door." Someone whose hair was covered with something like a shower cap, peered at me. Wake up! It's all over now.

Am I alive? I asked.

Of course, said the shower cap.

A loud boom rattled the window panes. What a storm, said the shower cap. I knew it was Saint Peter laughing.

Pearly White Yarn

Though strong and flexible now, Beryl knew that, too soon, her long, slender fingers could be bent and stiffened by age. Her fortieth birthday was fast approaching.

The knitting needles moved quickly, click-clacking as they wove pearly white yarn into delicate patterns. Occasionally, tears leaked from Beryl's eyes, wetting the yarn and making the needles slippery. She dropped a stitch making it necessary to undo a whole row and reknit it.

For almost two weeks, she had spent most of her time sitting in an armchair near the fireplace. Her hands and arms ached from knitting, yet she continued, rarely stopping to do anything else. She had visited the shops twice to purchase more yarn. Her husband pleaded with her to stop. "You seem to have lost your mind," he said. "You must overcome your disappointment."

Her only reply was, "I know what I must do, William."

The night grew late. Exhausted, William went to bed fearing tomorrow when he would call a doctor. His wife would surely be locked away.

Beryl put her knitting aside while she prodded the fire with an iron poker then added more wood. She sighed as she sat down again. A pile of small delicate pearly white blankets lay on a side table next to her. She didn't know how many more she must make. Outside, the wind sang an eerie tune and blew smoke back down the chimney.

She was weary. Her hands and arms still ached and her head had been throbbing for an hour. Her heart ache was much older.

They saw many physicians, at first hopeful because doctors could perform miracles these days, couldn't they? With each shake of a professional head and each "Nothing more can be done", spoken in a well-modulated voice, their hopes crumbled like autumn leaves. After a while, William became matter of fact, resumed his cheerfulness and got on with life. Beryl couldn't accept that she would never bear a child. She didn't care to adopt.

She bent to take another ball of yarn from a basket at her feet. She cast on stitches for a new blanket and remembered.

Almost two weeks ago, she woke in the night and thought William's snoring had disturbed her but his breathing was soft and regular. Then a hand gently stroked her brow. Her Grandmother stood by the bed. "There is still time," the old woman said.

"Time is running out," Beryl replied.

"Before you have a child of your own, you must do something for children in need."

Beryl sat up in bed. "What can I do, Grandmother?"

"Knit."

"Knit?"

"Yes. Knit. Use pearly white yarn and knit small, delicately patterned blankets. You will know when to stop. Keep the last one and give the rest to orphans." The old woman vanished and the only sound in the room was William's breathing.

Beryl didn't tell anyone about her Grandmother's visit for it had been ten years since the old woman's funeral. Others would think her insane.

Now weariness robbed Beryl's concentration. Several

times, she almost fell asleep. Then she succumbed and her knitting slipped to the floor.

The fire was dying and wind still blew smoke down the chimney when Beryl next raised her drooping head. Across her lap lay a small pearly white blanket. Knitted into the centre was a pattern of a sleeping infant. Beryl carefully laid the blanket on the chair then quietly slipped into bed next to her husband. She thought Wilbur or Wilma would be a suitable name.

Not Quite Perfect

There was no occasional lazy breeze or passing puff of wind bringing relief to the heat scorched city. Night came with a clammy cloak of oppression. Bodies soaked in sour smelling sweat, people lay exhausted in their beds. Some lay naked. Others, wishing a degree of decorum, lay under sweat dampened sheets.

Though a bit thin, Elizabeth's body was almost perfect. Her flesh was firm and her breasts had not yet begun to droop. She'd had lovers before she was married and now when widowed, but she was particular about who may gaze upon her naked body. She wore long cotton pyjamas and slept under a sheet, ignoring the fact that anyone wishing to catch a glimpse of her would need to climb up a drain pipe to reach the high window.

Her sleep was restless, with dreams of past and future mistakes. She also dreamed of finding a new lover though she knew she was not yet ready. Lapsing into deeper sleep, her dreams turned to fields of daffodils and apple orchards.

A change in the clammy atmosphere woke her. She was cold. Very cold. A stench which she knew was that of death occupied the space around her bed. In the darkness, something moved. As though she didn't know the answer to the question, she called out. "Who is there?"

A dark figure stood next to her bed and, for what seemed an eternity, stared at her with sunken, accusing, angry eyes. Slowly, an arm was raised and a finger pointed at her.

"Get away!" Elizabeth hissed. There was a show of uneven, yellowed teeth just before the figure disappeared. The stench of death remained.

A heaviness settled in the pit of her stomach as she turned on the light and checked all the windows and doors. They were all securely locked. She never went to bed without making sure of this.

She didn't want to return to her bedroom and the stench of death so she lay curled up on a small couch in the living room. Thoughts twirled and twisted in her head till just before dawn when she fell into a deep sleep.

She woke with a cricked neck and wondered why she wasn't in her bed, then trembled with fear as she remembered. She should be at work, she had a shop to run, but her staff would have to manage without her today.

She needed coffee and headache tablets. Her hands shook as she held a glass under the kitchen tap. The water came out in a thin dribble, as if there was something wrong with the plumbing. As she watched, the water turned grey, forming the shape of a distorted face with hollow, accusing black eyes. The glass fell from her hand.

"Why are you doing this? It's been two years!" Her voice was more of a scream than a shout. The face slid out of sight, down the plug hole but Elizabeth sensed the eyes still watching her. The water gurgled "Murderer, murderer, murderer," until she turned off the tap.

It was not hard to find her way to his grave. She had witnessed the lowering of his casket into it. She had procured the marble tomb stone engraved with "David Hendricks. 1972-2012." "In loving memory" wasn't included. Love had died long before.

Her scalp and the nape of her neck prickled under her

long hair. Beads of sweat gathered on her brow and upper lip. Her armpits were wet. She crouched in the dust near the grave then rose, deciding that what she had to do was best done standing. A workman with a wheelbarrow stopped and asked, "Are you all right?"

Exhaustion and heat had made her a bit wobbly on her feet. "I'm fine, thank you."

The man lifted the bottom of his shirt and mopped his face. "Visiting here is sometimes a bit hard. Don't stay too long in the sun." He continued on his way.

Elizabeth stared at the grave, "It's no use punishing me. Do you hear?"

It was difficult to tell if it was her thoughts or a voice from beneath the marble. "All I wanted was one more fix. Just one."

"I was trying to help. I was sick of your drugs and what they were doing to you and to me."

"You left me to die like a dog."

A distorted face on a long thin neck slithered up the side of the marble. The mouth didn't move but it was screaming obscenities and accusations. Over and over, she told him that he caused his own death but doubts clouded her mind. Perhaps she could have got him another fix. Perhaps he wouldn't have died then. She pushed the thoughts away. The motionless mouth cried, "You killed me as surely as sticking a knife in my heart."

A hand and arm, scrawny and dotted with festering puncture marks, appeared and reached towards her. "Go away!" she shouted. It disappeared.

The arguing continued. His voice grew fainter, less accusing.

The workman found her staring into space, mumbling about the need for self-responsibility. Elizabeth sensed it was best to play along with the Ambulance Officers' belief that she was confused.

At the hospital, doctors said she had heat stroke and was hallucinating. Elizabeth knew the truth. She would return to the grave and subdue that angry, lost soul; render speechless the unmoving mouth and seal those accusing eyes beneath the marble for ever. Only then would she be free to find a new lover worthy of gazing on her not quite perfect body.

Ted's Turkey

Most people in the district knew about Ted's turkey. In town, it had become a frequent topic of conversation in the pubs, shops, the barber's and on street corners. "Ted's turkey must be looking good," people would say or else they'd ask, "Have you seen Ted's turkey lately?"

Ted had bought the turkey and its cage at a country market. When his wife saw it, she asked "What are you going to do with that scrawny thing?"

"Well, Molly old girl," he said, "first of all I'm gonna build a pen for this here turkey then I'm gonna fatten him up then you're gonna cook him for Christmas dinner."

Molly wiped her hands on her apron. "You must be senile if you think you can fatten that thing up and I am certainly not planning to slave over a hot stove on Christmas Day. We will have a cold meal as usual."

"Well, you can cook him a few days early." Ted went off to buy steel posts and wire netting.

With plenty of food, Ted's turkey was soon no longer scrawny. He became a fine specimen strutting around his pen making, "Gobble gobble" noises and showing off his red wattles. Ted invited just about everyone he met to come and view the Christmas dinner he would share with his missus, the kids and grandkids.

Molly was determined she would not be providing a hot roast dinner for Christmas day. After all, this was Australia, not England. Something else was bothering her.

She had grown used to seeing the turkey in his pen at

the bottom of the garden and rather liked his gobble gobble noises and she thought he looked rather majestic and beautiful as he strutted around his small kingdom. He would eat from her hand and thanked her each time. She was beginning to dislike the idea of roasting and eating him. She tried to tell herself it would be different once Ted had chopped his head off and plucked out his feathers and that it would look just like any other turkey bought from the butcher. She still felt uneasy.

Christmas grew nearer, the turkey grew bigger while Molly became quiet and short tempered. Ted said, "I think you need a holiday, a bit of a change. We could go to Tasmania after Christmas." Molly made no comment.

A week before Christmas, Ted placed a big block of wood in a corner of the turkey pen. The turkey surveyed it from a distance but didn't go near it.

Then Ted bought a new axe from the hardware store. As he sat on the back step sharpening it, he said, "You know Molly that turkey has grown into such a big bugger you will have to help me hold it while I chop off its head." He whistled a few bars of "It's Beginning To Look A Lot Like Christmas" and didn't notice the colour drain from Molly's face. Then he said, "I will chop the bugger's head off the day after tomorrow so we can have cold roast turkey for Christmas."

On the morning of Christmas Eve, the butcher was surprised to see Ted walk into his shop. G'day Ted. How's that turkey?"

Ted's face and voice bore no Christmas cheer. "The bloody bird has escaped. Buggered if I know how. Maybe some bastard stole it. You wouldn't have a spare turkey or a leg or ham, would you?"

At home, he said to his wife, "I'm sorry about the turkey love. I know you were looking forward to a slice or two of roasted home grown turkey."

Molly didn't seem at all perturbed. She patted Ted's shoulder. "Never mind. We will make do with what we've got."

On Christmas day, all the creatures at the Scrubby Creek Animal Refuge got extra helpings of food. Strutting around in a big pen was a majestic looking turkey emitting gobble gobble sounds.

Secrets

The shabby room had once been elegant. Now the carpet was threadbare in places, the drapes faded and sagging and cobwebs hung from the ceiling. Through the cracked and dusty window pane, Scarlet watched yellow bulldozers and excavators hack earth and stone in an old city block that had probably seen more death than most modern wars. The machinery was surely unearthing and maybe destroying secrets connected to the terrible crime that had been committed in the very room where she stood. Would the connection be discovered? Was it better to leave some secrets buried?

She inched her way past the body lying on the floor. The naked body of a man whose white sagging flesh declared that he was no longer young. The body of a man, whose face had gaping, bloodied holes where there were once eyes.

She saw no one as she hurried down the stairs and out a side door, but she knew she was being watched. They would want to make sure she had got the message.

They hadn't wanted her to sell the properties, even though they'd had plenty of time to remove things; to remove evidence. She had promised herself that she wouldn't let them ruin her life. Those old buildings, including the hotel where the dead man lay, were her inheritance. It was her right to sell them.

The street was filled with noise and dust from the excavators. Ahead, someone leaned against a building. Another person stood at a corner. She was afraid, in fact, terrified. And angry.

Her father's business was not something she had involved herself in. She never asked questions, never interfered so why couldn't they leave her alone? Perhaps she should not have ignored the rumours about torture and murder in the basement of old warehouses.

Perhaps she should have asked questions when she heard comments about some mysterious eye. She remembered snatches of conversation. "Give him the eye." "He come good after he got the eye." She wondered if it meant the evil eye. Then, a few days after she put the properties on the market, she found an anonymous package it at her front door. It contained a typed note in capital letters, "STOP THE SALE." There was no signature, no address. Nothing to identify the sender, except for an eye, animal or human, she couldn't tell. The brown pupil was dull and staring. The white was turning yellow.

She changed her address, even changed her job. She had nightmares about the secrets that might be hidden in those buildings. She had nightmares about eyes. Dead eyes; eyes watching her, peering through keyholes and cracks. She thought of going to the police but feared the consequences. If she did that, maybe one of her own eyes would act as a warning to someone else.

Scarlet was stubborn. She would not give in. She'd let the sale go ahead. Whatever secrets lay in the old buildings would either be destroyed for ever or be discovered and reported to the police by someone else. Meanwhile, she would move to another city. Eventually, she might move to Spain. She had always fancied living in Spain.

The phone call from her real estate agent took her by surprise. He sounded anxious, strange, and mysterious. He insisted on meeting her in room 420 on the fourth floor of the old hotel. He said there were a few details to discuss before the sale of the building could be finalised. Now his body, without clothes, without eyes, lay on the floor of that room.

Scarlet tried to run but her legs felt heavy. Her heart beat very fast and her mouth was dry. She needed to sit down but there was no protection here on the street. She turned a corner and stumbled into a small, shabby cafe where she ordered a milkshake. The thick, cold liquid might cool and comfort her mouth and body and give her time to think.

With shaking hands, she held the straw to her lips and slowly drank the milk shake. There were sounds of sirens in the street and she realized the bulldozers and excavators were silent. Secrets were being uncovered.

On the pretext of going to the toilet, Scarlet left through the back door. The police were sure to want to interview her, but, tomorrow she would start the arrangements to move to Spain.

Smelling of Roses

Sandy lay curled into a ball, wrapped in the red blanket. He had made a bed and a shelter of sorts from cardboard cartons. A prefabricated house and flat pack furniture. He smiled at the thought and hoped there would be no gusts of wind during the night.

He was well used to tiredness but never before had he felt so exhausted. Some evil thing had settled in his lungs, fighting him for the right to breathe and leaking energy from his body. The old overcoat he wore was bunched up under his hip. Wriggling around to free it caused such a fit of violent coughing he wondered if it had been worth the effort.

The blanket blocked out some of the stench from nearby overflowing garbage bins. If he had cared to look, he may have found something edible amongst the garbage. He hadn't cared to look. He didn't have much of an appetite these days.

The smell of an unwashed body and spilled food and something much sweeter permeated the thinning threads of the blanket. The spilled food, dust, grit and bits of grass helped to hold the threads together. Sandy fell asleep with the rough texture against his face, the smell of roses the only thing that filled his nostrils.

Other memories had become dim and distorted; some had vanished but he would never forget Molly. He remembered her face as clearly as when he first met her on a bitter winter day. She gave him a red blanket and said there were no vacant beds. "God bless you", she said as she brushed tears from her eyes. The blanket was thick and soft and smelled of newness.

He wanted to tell her he didn't believe in God but he hadn't the heart to rebuff her kindness. Looking at her name badge, he said, "Thank you, Sister Molly."

"Just call me Molly." Her kind smile was something he rarely saw. It gave him a warm feeling, a feeling he liked.

As the years passed, there would sometimes be a vacant bed. Sometimes Molly wasn't there but Sandy felt her spirit and smelt her rose perfume. Molly never judged or criticised. In summer, she would wash his red blanket and hand it back smelling of roses.

Sandy became more and more accustomed to living on the streets. In spite of this, often, as he lay under a bridge or a park bench, he longed for a soft bed and a warm shower. Then, when he got lucky, he found the soft bed uncomfortable and the need of others to make conversation annoying. Whenever a well-meaning person offered to find him somewhere permanent to live, he took a train to the other side of the city and stayed a while.

Molly didn't try to find him a place of his own. She merely smiled, washed his blanket and gave him some fresh clothes. The stamp of old age grew more visible with each passing year. Her hair turned grey and wispy, crinkles crept on to her face and her hands trembled. Her eyes still smiled and she still smelled of roses.

The last time he saw her, she walked with a shuffle and carried a walking stick. She gave him a bowl of soup and said, "That old cough you've got worries me."

"Perhaps you could pray for me, Molly." He was startled by his own words. When had he decided to believe in God?

She smiled. "I pray for you each day." A warm feeling flooded his chest next to his raspy lungs.

A few weeks later, Sandy had a sudden feeling of dread. Somehow, he knew he must see Molly, though he wouldn't ask for a bed or a meal.

The journey took longer than usual because his chest rattled with every laboured breath and spasms of coughing almost brought him to his knees. The place was hushed, the staff sombre. They told him Molly had taken a turn for the worst last week and had gone to meet her maker two hours ago.

The garbage collectors came early in the morning. They tossed the cardboard shelter into the garbage truck and looked at the old red blanket. "That filthy thing smells of roses," one said as he lifted the blanket with the toe of his boot.

Sandy lay curled in a ball, his eyes closed. He no longer coughed; his chest no longer rattled; he no longer breathed. His lips formed a peaceful smile. One of the garbos said, "Poor old bloke must have been planning to meet someone special up there."

 # Old Grandmother 

A light breeze blowing across the Indian Ocean did little to comfort the citizens of Darwin wilting in the humid air. It was mid January but the monsoonal rains hadn't arrived. Year after year, the knowledge that the "wet" would soon arrive helped Darwinians endure the oppressive heat of November and early December. Now they were losing heart and beginning to despair. Some talked of moving south where it would be cooler.

The water at Berry Springs and Howard Springs were stagnant pools, unfit for swimming. Even the natural spring way down south at Elsey Station had dried up.

Stinging jelly fish abounded in the water at Fannie Bay and other Darwin beaches. Not that Sarah wanted to swim. She'd had her eighty fifth birthday last October and her swimming days were long gone.

She sat on the steps of the big old house in West Street, and fanned herself with a straw hat. She'd hardly ventured much further for weeks. Mary, her daughter in law, forbade it. "It's much too hot, Mother. Wait until its cooler."

Mary was always fussing around, insisting Sarah have another cup of water or else draping a wet cloth around her neck. Sarah's son, George, was no better. Just the same, she loved them dearly.

As if she knew what Sarah had been thinking, Mary appeared, face flushed with heat. Using her apron to wipe perspiration from her forehead and said,"I've taken a batch of scones from the oven. There's some plum jam left so I thought I'd make us a pot of tea."

"That sounds nice. Why don't you bring it out here? It's much cooler than the kitchen."

Like his father before him, George was a carpenter. He was retired but liked to keep his hand in. That morning, he'd gone to help a young cove build a house at Fannie Bay, so the women were alone in the house.

They sat in quiet companionship, sipping tea and eating scones. Sarah spoke. "I haven't been to the cemetery for ages. The graves are being neglected."

Mary too another sip of tea. "I'll get George to hitch Cobber to the buggy and take you there on Sunday."

"Don't be silly! It's just down the road. I can take myself there."

"Not in this heat. You now, I am sure I can smell rain."

"Oh, I hope you are right..."

Sarah was interrupted by the appearance of her great grandson, Tom. Strong as an ox, he stood six feet tall. He wore a sleeveless flannel shirt and patched dungarees. His feet were encased in a pair of dusty size twelve boots. Unruly brown hair poked from beneath a dirty felt hat. Agitated, his words tumbled out in a rush. "Hello Gran and old Grandmother. I need some help."

"What on earth is wrong?" Mary asked.

"It's Ellen," he said. "The baby's coming and she's having trouble. She said to fetch you, Gran. Her mother's there but doesn't seem to know what to do. Ellen said you'd know because you have helped with so many babies."

Mary gathered up towels and linen before hurrying off with Tom. They both reminded Sarah to stay cool and drink plenty of water. "There's beef in the in the cool safe so you can make a sandwich for lunch," Mary said as she left.

Sarah watched as they disappeared down the dusty street. I don't know what's wrong with young people. I had six of my own without any help.

She filled an empty sarsaparilla bottle with water, placed the straw hat on her head and collected her battered brown hand bag from her bedroom door knob. The cemetery was not far away. If she took her time, she could walk there without any difficulty.

Dark clouds were gathering to the east and Sarah saw flickers of lightning in the sky. The heat and humidity seemed to intensify as she walled. By the time she passed through the gate to the cemetery, her blue cotton dress clung to her back; perspiration trickled between her breasts and her long skirt made her legs feel as though they were in a furnace.

Taking a swig of water from the sarsaparilla bottle, she gazed at the graves set among rocks and gravelly red soil. Her parents, Ned and Eliza, lay next to each other. The inscription on Ned's grave extolled him as a good man who had built, among other things, Government House. The inscription on Eliza's grave spoke of her charity and kindness. Nearby were the graves of Nellie and Charles, two of Sarah's siblings who had died as infants.

A little further away, was the grave of Sarah's husband, Jack. Waiting for her, was a vacant plot next to him.

She took from her handbag some pearly white shells, collected from the beach back when the weather was cool. Stooping, she placed some on the infants' graves. "I thought you would like these pretty shells. I haven't visited for a while but I haven't forgotten you." She felt a bit dizzy as she straightened up. Must be the heat. She had another sip of water.

Lightning slashed the darkening sky over Fannie Bay as Sarah turned to her father's grave. "Your great great grandson is a fine young fellow who is a builder like you. Now he is all in a tiz because his wife is having a baby." She placed some shells on his grave.

Turning to her mother's grave, she felt the dizziness again. In the centre of the grave, she arranged some shells in the shape of a flower. "There you are, Mum. You always liked flowers and shells."

Then she placed a large shell, pearly white and unblemished, on her husband's grave. "I still miss you, my Darling." As she sat on the edge of the grave, she was overcome by a great weariness. A searing pain gripped her chest. She cried out as thunder roared in anger behind the heavy, dark clouds.

Not far away, a young woman, drenched in perspiration, made a noise that was half scream, half grunt and a tiny new human being was expelled unceremoniously from her body. The red and slimy infant emitted a loud "Laah, laah."

Mary said, "It's a girl."

Her face streaked with tears of happiness and the echo of pain, the young woman said, "I will name her Sarah after Old Grandmother."

Sarah clutched her chest and leaned against the tombstone. She cried out in a thin reedy voice and breathed no more. The brim of her straw hat sagged and her sodden clothes clung to her body in the monsoonal rain.

Someplace in Paradise

Muriel surveyed the tray of dainty sandwiches, the array of iced tea cakes, the chocolates, gleaming silverware, delicate china and starched white napery. She hadn't wanted to come here but her daughters insisted. These days, they treated her more and more as though she didn't know her own mind.

"Have another sandwich, Mother." Audrey was the worst of the three.

Monica filled Muriel's tea cup without asking and Meredith leaned across the table and straightened her collar. "Yes. Eat up. You don't turn eighty-nine every day."

They were all good, decent women and it was good of them to bring her to this place for high tea, but Muriel would have preferred to eat cakes at home. She had come here once with Harry for dinner when they were still courting. He was so handsome and they were so much in love! She remembered how they had gazed into each other's eyes as they sipped sweet wine. Afterwards, they had danced.

Monica was excitedly talking about her forthcoming holiday in Venice. "Your father and I had a marvellous time there. Be sure to take a gondola ride." Muriel did her best to make conversation but everything brought back so many memories it was hard to concentrate.

She couldn't remember when she first realized she and Harry had fallen out of love. It was a slow, sneaky process. The heat of passion dwindled away until all that remained was cold ashes. Still, she had been a good and dutiful wife. She'd had one brief fling with a plumber when Harry was away on a business trip and the children were staying with country cousins for school holidays.

"You're not listening, Mother. Are you tired?" Meredith offered her another cake.

"Thank you, dear. I guess I am a bit tired."

She had worn new shoes when she danced the night away with the plumber. Beautiful, high heeled gold coloured sandals. She still had them somewhere.

Audrey was taking charge, as usual. "We will get you home soon so you can have a rest. We will have to start packing up your things."

"Oh, I'm not in a hurry to pack. I'm still not sure about moving into that serviced apartment in the retirement village."

Now it was Meredith, "Well Dad's not around anymore and you can't be expected to do everything on your own." They always thought they knew what was best for her, what she really wanted.

She missed Harry. They had never talked much but had grown comfortable with each other. He dealt with home repairs and heavy stuff and she attended to domestic tasks. She knew he'd had more than one affair. She had a good nose for the smell of another woman. She didn't know if he had guessed about her dalliance with the plumber. He noticed the shoes and said, "I've never seen you wear those."

She replied, "They are kind of special."

The plumber had been special. His strong arms held her close as they twirled around the dance floor. She relaxed in his embrace and something wild was released inside her. They spent the night in a motel room doing things that made her smile and blush even now. The next weekend, they had gone to a seaside cottage and done more of the same. She never once regretted her actions.

It was late afternoon when Muriel's daughters took her home, saying they'd be back in two days to start packing. Muriel fell asleep on a recliner chair. She forgot about dinner.

It was night when she woke. She went to her bedroom and crawled under her bed. The sandals were covered in dust. She cleaned them on an old skirt from her wardrobe. They still fitted her feet, though her bunions poked through the straps. She was no longer used to wearing heels so she practised walking around the bed.

In the living room, she put some CDs in the CD player. Jazz music. It was hard to dance on carpet so she went out onto the veranda. The moon bathed her in light as she danced. Her feet remembered the steps. Her body remembered the plumber. Her sandals slid across the floor and she swayed to the rhythm of the music. The tempo quickened and she moved faster and faster, twirling and swaying from one end of the veranda to the other and back again. She was not aware of the blisters on her feet or the pain in her calf muscles. The music and the memory of the plumber had taken her to Paradise.

Her daughters came when Muriel didn't answer her phone. Tearfully, Monica said, "I never saw Mother wearing those shoes. They must have meant something special to her."

The End of the Kitchen Bench

Edna's joints were quite stiff these days, especially her hips. Even though it had been months ago, she hadn't fully recovered from surgery on her right hip. Struggling to remove her shoes, she wondered if it would be easier to roll into bed fully clothed. She supposed she might sleep better if she at least removed her shoes.

Using long tongs, she managed to remove her shoes and poke them out of the way while she tackled her socks. She was eager to take a shower; to stand under hot running water and feel some of the pain and stiffness wash away. It would be worth the effort of undressing. Afterwards, slipping on a nightdress would be relatively easy.

Fifteen minutes later, Edna stepped into the shower recess with her left leg and dragged her right leg after it. Standing to one side, she turned on the hot water tap and tested its temperature with one hand. Tepid. She turned the tap a bit more. Tepid. She turned the tap on fully. Still tepid. By now, she was shivering. "Tepid is better than cold," she told herself. Hurriedly, she washed her upper body then used a sponge on a long stick to wash her lower legs and feet. She would need to look at the hot water system tomorrow. There was no use in asking Jonas because he was unreliable.

Before dragging herself and her right leg into bed, Edna wrote a note on the back of a torn envelope. It was just two words. "Hot water." She placed it on top of all the other reminder notes spread across one end of the kitchen bench. She would be sure to see it in the morning.

Jonas was snoring when Edna finally manoeuvred into bed. She didn't disturb him.

She was woken the next morning by Petrov, the big black and white cat smacking her face with his paw. She had overslept and Petrov wanted his breakfast. He was not a cat to be kept waiting. On occasions, he had used his claws or his teeth if his needs were not swiftly met. Edna often wondered why she had bothered rescuing the ungrateful beast from the animal shelter. The two dogs of indeterminate breed were not much better. They would be eager to be let out of the laundry.

Sighing, Edna manoeuvred out of bed, waking Jonas in the process. She donned a floral dressing gown and shoved her feet into pink slippers worn down at the heels.

Petrov beat her to the kitchen and leapt onto the bench, scattering reminder notes all over the floor. "Now look what you've done, you stupid cat!" She shouted. The cat meowed and swiped at her with a paw. "Oh be patient!"

She set a dish of cat food on the floor. Petrov sent a few more notes flying as he jumped from the bench. Edna went to let the dogs out. She would have to pick up the notes and sort them out. "Stupid cat!"

She set out coffee mugs, turned on the electric kettle and was putting two slices of bread in the toaster when Jonas appeared. He had a bit of tissue paper stuck to his chin. "Cut myself shaving," he said. "Must be something wrong with the hot water service."

Edna was busily grabbing up notes from the kitchen floor with her long tongs and paid little attention to Jonas. "You will have to get a wriggle on if you don't want to be late for your meeting."

"I know." Jonas buttered a piece of toast and shoved most of it in his mouth. He seemed grumpy.

Edna was having trouble sorting out the notes. Some were written on scraps of newspaper. Some bits of paper were covered with her almost indecipherable small writing, even up the sides of the paper. She dumped them all on the bench and sat down to have breakfast. She had a lot to do today and must hurry.

As she washed her face in the bathroom, Edna noticed that the water was tepid. She wrote a reminder note to do something about it and put the note on the kitchen bench.

It took quite a while to get dressed, especially getting her right leg into things. She could have done with a rest after all that effort but she had to go to the library and she was meeting someone for lunch. With a certain amount of movement, her hip and other joints loosened up a bit. Too much movement and everything went on strike, so she had to be careful. A walking stick might help. She wrote a note to remind her to Google walking sticks. She placed the note on the end of the kitchen bench.

That evening, as usual, Jonas was first to go for a shower. A few minutes later, he bellowed, "There's no hot water. It's barely tepid."

Edna wrote a reminder note and placed it on the end of the kitchen bench.

Three's a Crowd

An occasional gust of wind did nothing to spoil Fred's pleasure as he leaned back on a wooden bench outside the butcher shop. He might have dozed in the warm sunshine if he wasn't so interested in the comings and goings on the street. He should have been on his way home with the sausages and bread Lola had sent him to buy, but the street was far more entertaining than Lola's nagging.

Passers-by stopped to yarn about the weather or ask if he could keep an eye on their dog while they dashed into the bakery. Women came out of the beauty parlour patting the stiffened hair on their heads and touching their waxed chins.

Swept along by the wind, a plastic bag wrapped itself around Fred's leg. As he shook his leg he noticed something in the bag. He looked at it with unbelieving eyes. A ten dollar bill. Furtively he slipped it into a trouser pocket. He peered around to see if anyone was searching their handbag or wallet or pocket. No one was acting as though they had lost something. No one frowned and searched the footpath. Just the same, Fred felt a tinge of guilt somewhere deep inside him.

He wondered if he should give the money to a charity; some organization that helped the homeless or fed the hungry. That kind of thought didn't stay with him very long. In fact, it had hardly settled when he remembered that he'd been down on his luck a few times and never sought charity. He had nearly always paid his way and only cheated when there was no option. He was just as deserving as the next one. He decided to drop into the pub and have a beer. Lola would never know.

He heard a familiar voice. "Hello Fred. How are you?"

It was young Tom, a cheeky, harmless sort of fellow who was always ready to be in on a prank. They chatted for a while about the new Prime Minister and how Asians were pushing up the price of real estate. Tom sat down next to Fred. "You wouldn't happen to have that twenty quid I loaned you a few months ago would you?"

"If you don't mind waiting for the rest, I can give you ten quid now." Fred reached into his pocket, trying to smile.

"Thanks mate. That's start" Tom whistled as he strode to his car. On his way home, he stopped at Dora's flower stall and bought two bunches of red rises for ten dollars. One was for his wife. The other was for a brunette called Suzie who he would visit later instead of doing the extra shift he had told his wife about. That way, he could keep both women happy.

Dora put the $10 in her cash box with the rest of the takings for the day. She smiled as she thought of her healthy bank account. One more week and she could fulfil her dream. Her scoffing husband believed she was making only "pocket money" from her flower stall. He scoffed at most things she did. He was in for a big surprise. She planned to leave him a note.

Dear Patrick, remember the Spaniard who served us drinks in that Carlton pub? The handsome fellow who was on a working holiday? The one you said was probably gay? Well, I'm meeting him in Madrid and he isn't gay. Couldn't invite you because two's company and three's a crowd.

The Philosopher

Trevor glanced through the tree tops at the starry night sky before crouching to strike a match. The yellow flame licked at a pile of dry leaves and twigs and a small spiral of smoke rose into the air. With great care, Trevor gradually added larger sticks then solid wood until the fire was sufficient to cook his meal. He would dine on potatoes and a fish he had caught at sunset. He sat on a fold up canvas chair and contemplated his good fortune. A soft breeze blew across the Timor Sea, cooling the humid air and rustling leaves. He was not discomforted by the sense that he was surrounded by creatures of the night. There was something peaceful and spiritual about this place.

In the distance, curlews began their ritual of screaming. Trevor smiled, wondering how such an insignificant grey bird could make such a noise. Some people didn't like the sound of the curlew but Trevor wasn't bothered by it. He'd been partially deaf since childhood. That bothered him. He had never been able to fully participate in society. On the positive side, he'd learned to be philosophical, learned to be comfortable with his own company. Furthermore, loud noises rarely worried him.

He prodded the fish then the fire with a stick. He used a fork to prod the potatoes. He sighed. He'd found a peaceful, solitary haven, at least for a while.

After his meal, he cleaned his dishes in the ocean. His wife, Shirley, wouldn't have approved. Not now. There was a time when she would have laughed and hugged him but such things were but a shadow of a memory. They had grown up together, he and Shirley. She understood about his deafness and need for solitude though she sometimes lost patience with his philosophising. She was a woman of action.

There was no need for a fire on such a warm night but he added more wood. The dancing yellow and orange flames were mesmerizing and soothing, the smoke smelling of eucalypt. He boiled a billy can of water for tea.

They were soul mates for a long time. Her practicality and his philosophy worked in harmony. The harmony began to unravel after the twins were born. He didn't hear them crying at night. He told his frazzled wife things would get better, the joy of watching the boys grow would compensate for sleepless nights. She didn't want philosophy. She wanted action, relief, sleep. Instantly. He tried to be more helpful, more practical but the damage was done. The twins were the thread holding the marriage together and it became more frayed with each passing year.

Trevor sipped a mug of sweet black tea as he watched a burst of sparks rise from the fire. Unconsciously, he rubbed at a twinge in his right shoulder. He had injured his shoulder working as a concreter and ignored the pain until he could no longer work and his shoulder was beyond repair. He lost his philosophical outlook and his interest in most things. Eventually, he moved out, went on the road because he was making everyone miserable.

He made another mug of tea. He liked the mix of the sweet, sugary taste and the smell of the wood fire smoke. He sipped the scalding liquid and wondered if he should stay a few more days or move on tomorrow. Perhaps he would stay. He had grown tired of moving on.

The canvas chair wasn't comfortable but he fell asleep, his chin resting on his chest. He was woken by his mobile phone vibrating in his shorts pocket. The text message read, Hi Dad. Where r u? We miss u. School hols soon. Cn we visit u? Luv Rob n Joe.

With awkward, shaking hands, he fumbled to reply. Sure can. Darwin. Will contact soon. Luv Dad.

The fire spluttered and hissed as he dowsed it a billy can of water. He turned towards his swag. Tomorrow he would be moving on to a proper camping ground, buying a proper tent and a couple of fishing rods. A soft breeze blew in from the Timor Sea, stars twinkled in a cloudless sky, the curlews continued their chorus and he would be seeing his boys soon. What more could he want? As he fell asleep, his last thoughts were about whether or not Shirley might tag along with the boys.

The Likes of Vic

I was searching for my brother, Vic, when I last trod the streets of Sydney. In the stifling heat, my clothes clung to me while perspiration trickled down my back. The thunderstorms at night brought brief reprieve and washed away some of the fumes from the ceaseless traffic. They didn't help the plight of those who slept rough. The weather pays no heed to the likes of Vic.

Prostitutes competed for customers on street corners in Kings Cross. Torn net stockings and skimpy dresses barely covered their skeletal bodies. Intent on earning the price of their next heroin fix, they had no time to think of the likes of Vic. Walking to the Wayside Chapel, I stepped over more than a few people who had already scored that fix. Homeless souls lingering near the chapel knew Vic well. They said they hadn't seen him for a while but he was looking good back then.

I went down to Rushcutters Bay and stopped for a cool drink at the Royal Cruising Yacht Club. Several big yachts sailed in and moored next to the big wooden jetties, stirring a yearning in my soul. It had been far too long since I had sailed those very waters with my husband. Laughter broke my reverie as the yachting fraternity descended on the outdoor dining area. A jovial lot, wearing colour co-ordinated nautical clothes, they talked about Kevlar sails and high tech gear as if such things were throw away commodities. The yachting fraternity would probably prefer not to know the likes of Vic.

Woolamaloo, with its old wharves and warehouses converted into upmarket apartments and cafes, was vibrant and trendy. Wearing last summer's sales specials,

I felt out of place. That night, I dined on sea food at Cockle Bay and watched the reflected lights of Sydney dance in the waters of Sydney Harbour. Here, the city pulsed with life and panache but there was not one the likes of Vic dabbing the corners of their mouth with a linen napkin.

I visited my ancient cousin in Balmain and fell in love again with charming restored terrace houses. At the end of the street, there was once a wharf where many a ship, bearing wounds inflicted by Japanese submarines, limped home. Deaf as a post and losing her sight, my cousin was delighted by my visit. She is not much interested in wealth so cares not that her unrestored house with its outside toilet is worth a fortune. She would be happy to share her home with the likes of Vic but he would be too proud to accept such charity.

I paused to rest in leafy parks, travelled beneath the city streets on crowded trains and felt the sand of Bondi Beach beneath my toes. I took a ferry to Manly where I listened to jazz musicians in the square and watched drunken revellers emerge from the Styne Hotel. I ate fried noodles in China Town and melting ice cream at Circular Quay. In the doss houses of Darlinghurst and the refuges around Surrey Hills, I met many a fellow the likes of Vic. I never met up with my brother. If ever I am in Sydney again, I swear I will search more thoroughly.

The Maggot

The trial was due to begin tomorrow. Jack O' Dea planned to be there for every minute no matter how long it lasted. The man in the dock deserved to feel the full force of Jack's hatred for him.

Hector Fennessey would be found guilty regardless of what his solicitor and lawyer might say. They'd say Fennessey was a good man, that he was at home with his latest floozy at the time of the crime and there was no way he could be the guilty party.

When he was led to the dock, Fennessey wore a grey suit, blue shirt and matching striped tie. It was an attempt at making him appear to be a decent, law abiding citizen but he had always been a maggot and still was. He glanced around the courtroom and into the steely eyes of Jack O'Dea.

Five days a week for two weeks, Jack sat in the front row of the public gallery. He listened while the legal beagles played their game, trying to outwit and outdo each other, strutting around as though they were on the big screen. He listened while witnesses were called, questioned and cross examined. His eyes never left the maggot's face. Fennessey sat gazing at his hands. He knew that if he looked up, he would see the pure hatred in Jack's eyes. That's what Jack wanted him to see.

On the tenth day, when all the evidence had been presented and all the witnesses questioned and cross examined, the lawyer for the prosecution presented his summary. Hector Fennessey had committed a heinous crime. He hadn't expected Mabel O'Dea to be working in the back of her antique shop when he broke in late at night. Never one to let such things stand in his way, he bludgeoned her to death with a marble statuette before stealing valuable antiques.

The defence lawyer said Fennessey was known as a hardworking, good citizen who had never before faced court. In fact, he was so honest he had never been issued with a traffic infringement fine. His fiancé, whom he planned to marry soon, had testified that he had spent the night in question with her.

It was up to the jury to decide if Fennessey would walk free or go to prison. The verdict was unanimous. Guilty.

Jack O'Dea's steely gaze was accompanied by a kind of sneering smile. He felt sweet revenge. Fennessey hadn't handed over half of the money from the bank robbery they committed together twelve years ago and he'd had a long standing affair with Mable. Now he was rid of both of them. For a little longer he would pretend to be the grieving widower. Then he could live the good life on Mabel's wealth. Meanwhile he must properly dispose of the blood splattered clothes he had hidden beneath the floor boards.

Shower Cap

There was a dirty ring where her favourite coffee mug usually sat on the kitchen bench. Cutlery and half a poached egg were on a plate in the sink. Her CDs were gone from the coffee table. Her side of the wardrobe was empty. A hint of French perfume hung in the air.

In the bathroom, the shower was dripping; a wet towel and a plastic shower cap, the kind you found in a $2 shop, lay on the floor.

Oscar thought Miranda had probably gone for good. He tried to pretend he didn't care. He tossed the wet towel in the laundry basket, stopped the drip and hung the cap on a hook on the wall, then wondered why he had done that. He had never worn a shower cap and was unlikely to do so.

He scraped the egg into the trash bin then washed and dried the cutlery and plate before putting them away. He wiped the kitchen bench but left the coffee mug ring. He didn't want to forget Miranda's untidiness.

When he first saw her, she was sitting on a park bench, dappled sunshine playing on her long brown hair, half of which had escaped from a jade clip on top of her head. She was reading a book and munching on an apple. She looked up and smiled as his passing shadow fell upon her. He knew he had found the woman of his dreams.

Their relationship began hesitatingly, as if they had something so pure and tender they were afraid to test its strength lest it break and be lost forever. As the months passed, their shared bond became like a perpetual spring, filled with sunshine, flowers and bird song.

Now, Oscar thought about dinner and remembered that he had never learned to cook. Miranda was a brilliant cook and, at first, this seemed to more than compensate for the trail of dirty dishes and cooking utensils she left in her wake.

He consulted the Yellow Pages and ordered take away pizza. It had been so long since he had eaten such food, he had forgotten the taste of rubbery cheese but supposed he'd just have to get used to it. At least there wouldn't be many dishes to clean.

He wiped grease from his lips with a paper serviette, wondering when their relationship had turned sour. There seemed to be no exact moment or day or week or month. It had happened slowly, like mould on bathroom tiles. You don't notice it until one day it seems to be everywhere, all green and black and slimy and you realize it didn't happen overnight. It grows a little bit at a time until it's suddenly there, right in your face.

"You've left your clothes on the floor again," he'd say. "Who cares?" she'd say.

"That music is terrible. It's giving me a headache," she'd say. "It's my favourite," he'd say.

To start, there had been a light heartedness about it all. They compromised. She tried to be tidy and he didn't play his music when she was around. Then other thorns of discontent arose. They argued about work schedules and whose turn it was to put out the trash. Their golden spring slid into a murky grey winter.

It was winter now. The dampness, the icy winds and the dreariness of it all seemed to meld with Oscar's very essence. The dreariness within was no longer discernable from the dreariness without.

He saw the shower cap each time he used the bathroom.

He hung a towel over it but knew it was still there. Miranda had worn it with her large ears sticking out. She looked ridiculous and he loved her all the more for it.

Winter morphed into spring. He was till dreary. He bought some recipe books and learned how to cook, ruining pots and pans along the way. He remembered Miranda saying. "It doesn't matter. I love cooking for you," as she fed him some tasty morsel from the end of her stirring spoon. He still didn't clean away the ring left by her coffee mug. He placed a drink coaster over it.

He dated a few girls and found them all wanting in some way. He brought one, a red head named Mavis, home to his bed. Things were going well until she twined her long, slim legs around his and he thought of Miranda's short, rather chubby legs. He faked a sudden attack of nausea and Mavis left without a word of sympathy.

A work colleague said, "I saw Miranda in a cafe the other day. She hadn't changed and the bloke she was with..." Oscar walked away. He didn't want to hear the rest. He wondered if the said bloke was picking up after her.

As spring turned to summer, he caught sight of her in a crowded art gallery. He had no time to speak to her because she turned a corner and was soon out of sight. Afterwards, he wondered what he would have said. "Let's find something to eat," as if they had never parted? Would she have replied, "Sure. Let's go," as if it was all arranged?

Summer came with its thunderstorms and humidity. Oscar's essence was still stuck in a murky winter. He moved the drink coaster on the kitchen bench and looked at the stain so out of place there on the clean, white bench. It was time for it to go. Wiping it with a sudsy cloth made no difference, nor did a good rub with an abrasive cleaner. He put the coaster back over it.

The doorbell rang and he went to answer it. Miranda

stood there, her hair spilling from a clip on the top of her head. She was alone. There was no bloke with her.

She looked up at him, her face framed between her large ears. "I've come for my shower cap."

He noticed she carried an overnight bag. "Why don't you stay the night?"

"Perhaps I will." Spring had started all over again.

From So High a Height

Icy wind whipped at her coat, freezing her stockinged legs. Strands of brown hair escaped from her head scarf, clinging to her eyes and mouth as if to blind and silence her. It was good that few people were on the streets at this late hour. They would only make things difficult.

She looked up. Buildings rose so high in the night sky she could barely see their tops. She craned her neck to find the tallest one of all and a wave of giddiness swept over her.

Leaning against a giant marble statue of a horse, she felt the coldness through the frozen flesh of her cheek. The horse would show her no kindness. The wind snatched away her scarf and sent it whirling and twisting between buildings. She watched it disappear, along with her spirit. Her hair was violently blown this way and that, trying to tear itself from her scalp.

Small and insignificant, she was like a piece of grit on the city street. But not invisible. The tall buildings and giant statues looked down on her. Looked down with scorn; with judgement. Even the stars, way up there in that cold night sky could see her guilt.

Swaying towards her, the tallest building beckoned. The foyer was deserted but an enormous jade urn watched as she pressed the elevator button. On the long journey up, the elevator moaned and hummed a prayer for the souls of the wicked.

She stepped out on the top floor and the elevator slid down, too quickly, as if pleased to be rid of her. The door to the balcony was unlocked.

Out here, the fierce wind forced her backwards. Gripping the balcony rail, she steadied herself and looked down, down, down. Surely a fall from so high a height would be fatal. She lifted one leg over the rail, then the other, teetered for a moment then let go.

The Oodnadatta Track

I vowed that, come September, we'd be gone. Our souls were wearied by the endless grey winter skies of this city. Our complexions had paled and our fingers numbed. We were tired of umbrellas and wet shoes and washing hung to dry before the heater.

We'd have left earlier but for the neighbour's cockatoo. Foolishly, we agreed to care for Henry Featherstone while the neighbours took a three month romp around Italy and France and Spain. Now we were fed up with hearing "I'm Henwee Featherstone." I had taken to correcting him. "Henry, not Henwee." It made no difference. We were sick of hearing. "Answer the phone. Answer the phone," or "That's the doorbell." We weren't deaf.

The neighbours were returning in August. Come September, we'd be gone where our shoes stayed dry and the sun bronzed our skin; where cockatoos lived in trees and didn't have fancy names.

It was our habit to depart for warmer climes when winter wrapped this most liveable city in a dripping embrace. We swapped traffic fumes mingled with ash from open fireplaces for the red dust of Coober Pedy mullock heaps, the dry heat of saltbush plains and the smell of a hot motor when we stopped at a remote rest place on an outback highway.

One July day, we drank a cappuccino at the Marla Roadhouse, thousands of kilometres from the most liveable city. We might have made our own coffee, the instant variety, but we liked to indulge ourselves now and then. Greasy chips, meat pies and dim sims were on offer but we chose cellophane wrapped fruit cake.

The coffee was passable though it lacked fancy artwork on the froth. Here, a couple of hundred kilometres down the road from Coober Pedy, the barista probably didn't get much practise. The cake was stale.

We sat outside, our backs turned to the threat of being fried by the morning sun. The sky was a cloudless blue dome. None of the squawking cockatoos in the nearby gum trees laid claim to a fancy name.

Road trains, brakes hissing, stopped to refuel and we wondered about the people who chose to live the life of a long haul truckie. Grey nomads emerged all stiff and limping from motor homes and four wheel drive vehicles. Some made themselves a cuppa and stood yarning in small groups. We brushed away flies and listened to talk of the price of fuel, busted axles, free camping spots and run down motels, kangaroos and road conditions. The driver of a vehicle powder coated in dust said the Oodnadatta Track from William Creek, on the edge of Lake Eyre, shook your bones and churned up the bacon and eggs you ate for breakfast.

"Now, that's a thought," said Will, rising from his chair, "We ought to churn up our breakfast one of these days."

"Sounds like fun," I replied. We wanted to visit every nook and cranny of Australia before we died. We had done well so far but we had never been on the Oodnadatta Track.

The next time we stopped at the Marla Roadhouse, the greasy chips, the meat pies, dim sims and cellophane wrapped fruit cake were still on offer but there was no cappuccino, just instant coffee with wooden stirrers for the sugar. The fellow behind the counter said the coffee machine was broken.

"That's a pity," I said, "Can you fix it?"

His face was crinkled at the corner of his dark eyes. He scratched his beard and looked directly at me. "Don't reckon so. We sent it to be fixed but it fell off the back of a truck somewhere along the Oodnadatta Track."

"Oh dear, "I said, "I suppose that's the end of it."

He scratched his beard again. "Well, with a bit of luck, we might get it back. There's a thousand dollar reward." His eyes were smiling but his face was straight.

I suspected he was pulling my leg. The Oodnadatta Track was over six hundred kilometres of dirt road and it seemed an unlikely route to send a coffee machine needing repair. Just the same, the reward was tempting but we had a schedule and the motor was losing oil.

I often thought of that coffee machine lying alone by the side of the track, its bubble wrap and cardboard box long since blown away. I pictured it all scratched and dinted in a pile of gibber stones or half buried in dirt near a stretch of the track where the soil was softer. I wondered if a camel had trampled it beneath great cloven hoofs. Maybe it was ever only a figment of imagination, a yarn spun for unsuspecting tourists from down south.

Winter descended on the city again and we had to stay for a wedding but, in September, we packed our gear and headed for the Oodnadatta Track. We thought we'd go to William Creek and maybe take a scenic flight over Lake Eyre. That dusty track shook our bone marrow but our feet were dry and the sun shone.

We came upon it by accident. We had stopped to film a couple of scrub turkeys when we spotted it half hidden beneath a clump of salt bush. It had a sideways twist, it had lost its shine and it was home to a family of mice. It was too big for us to move so we left it there in its lonely, dusty resting place.

The fellow at the Marla Roadhouse said there never was a coffee machine on the back of a truck somewhere along the Oodnadatta Track. It was just a yarn he told pale skinned southerners. We showed him a photo. He said, "That could have been taken indoors with just a few props." He said not to ask for a reward.

We know what we saw, what we touched even though some bearded man handing out wooden sugar stirrers would call us liars. Our outback journeys have taken on a new dimension as we watch for discarded and lost treasures among the gibber stones on a lonely desert track.

Through The Looking Glass

Jessica rested one foot on the other as she watched her mother purchase homemade jam and a butternut pumpkin from the market stall. She'd been told that, as a special treat, she could choose something for herself but there were so many wondrous things, she couldn't decide.

Her mother placed her purchases in a shopping basket. "Have you decided? The stall holders will soon be packing up." Jessica looked around at all the beautiful things. She wanted them all! How could she choose just one?

Then she saw something glittering in the sunlight. It was a looking glass, the prettiest she had ever seen. The frame and handle were the colour of the sky on a summer day. Set in it, were shiny pearls. She gazed at it in wonder. "It's the only one, Love," the fat woman behind the stall said.

Peering into the glass, Jessica saw her own chubby face and unruly red hair. She saw something else as well and instantly knew it was magic.

Later, Jessica helped her mother prepare some of the pumpkin and other vegetables for dinner, being careful not to cut her fingers with the potato peeler and knife. She tasted the new jam and licked the custard spoon. Between doing these things, she checked on the looking glass placed face up on the chair beside her bed. Something magical was sure to happen and Jessica didn't want to miss it.

At bedtime, Jessica's parents were too busy to read her a story, so, in her bright yellow pyjamas, she climbed into bed with her Pooh Bear book. She didn't mind that she didn't know some of the big words. She made up her own words. She had gotten to an exciting part where Pooh Bear had climbed up a tree and couldn't get down, when there was a noise beside her.

Turning, Jessica saw a girl who looked remarkably like herself except that the girl wore blue pyjamas embroidered with pearls.

"How did you get here?" Jessica asked.

"Through the looking glass, of course. What's your name?"

"Jessica. What's yours?"

"Myrtle Merkle. Let's play bouncing."

They bounced on the bed, bouncing higher and higher, almost bumping their heads on the ceiling. Squealing with laughter, they bounced onto the floor.

"What's all the noise?" Jessica's father stood in the doorway with a stern look on his face. Myrtle Merkle was gone. Jessica sat on the floor alone. "Pooh Bear pushed me onto the floor." Her father smiled as he tucked her back into bed.

After that, Myrtle Merkle, always dressed in blue, often came through the looking glass. They played hide and seek, held tea parties with Jessica's dolls and even made mud pies at the back of the garden. Sometimes they whispered secrets to each other or told scary stories that made them hide under the bed.

The little girl with the unruly carrot coloured hair clapped her hands and whirled around on one leg. "Oh! Grandma, that's the prettiest looking glass I have ever seen! Are you really, really, really giving it to me to keep?"

The Grandma prodded her own unruly grey hair into

place and smiled. "I am really, really really giving it to you to keep."

The girl ran her fingers over the pearls in the blue frame and peered at her reflection. "I think there is something magic in there."

The Grandma nodded. "Oh. I am sure there is."

The Spirit of Her Ancestors

"You lookin tired. Watsup?" Mary poured boiling water into two mugs. Her ebony skin showed signs of aging but her thin arms and hands were still strong.

"Can't sleep." Elke was thin and strong like her mother but her skin was a lighter shade and her nose not so broad.

"Why? Watsamatter?" they carried their coffee to the veranda and sat on the old couch, it's well-worn cushions moulding to the shape of their bodies.

Elke didn't answer but sat gazing out at the Indian Ocean, her face deep in thought.

"You hearin them spirits again?" Mary took a sip of her coffee.

"Nearly every night and sometimes early in the morning. It's real, Mum. I'm not imagining it."

"Better not letcha father hear ya talkin like that."

Elke thought of her father. She both loved and resented him. He had come to this country with his own culture and beliefs but dismissed many of the beliefs of the indigenous people. "Fairy stories for kids" he would say. Yet he had adapted well to this land and he enjoyed eating witchety grubs as much as the apple strudel he had taught Mary to bake. He was a good father and Elke didn't want to upset him.

"I won't say anything to Dad but I just know they are calling me." She finished drinking her coffee. "I'd better get on my way to work. See ya."

That evening, sitting on her own veranda, she heard it again, as she knew she would. The throbbing, vibrating sound of didgeridoos accompanied by a soft moaning and whispering. A sighing of sadness, a humming of wisdom and knowledge and the whispering of untold stories. A sound of beckoning and invitation. She felt something in the fibres of her being respond and she knew what she must do.

The journey was three days long. Her four wheel drive rattled over dust and stones, crossed dry rivers and splashed through water in others. Red dust swirled behind her as she traversed the harsh land.

At night, as she slept in rest spots by the roadside, the sound of didgeridoos and the chant of corroborees filled her dreams. The sweet musty smell of spinifex filled her nostrils.

It was late morning when she arrived at the community. Gulipi sat in the dust leaning against a giant boab tree. He could have fetched a chair from the house but he preferred to sit here. His tattered shorts were so dusty it was difficult to determine their colour. The rest of his body was naked. His skin was like wrinkled black leather, his limbs so thin they resembled sticks. White hair rimmed his bald scalp, a wispy white beard reached halfway down his chest. Bushy white eyebrows shaded his age faded brown eyes.

Elke sat in the dust with him and listened to him speaking all that day and the next. From time to time, others came to sit for a while. Some brought food and drink. As the hot sun moved across the sky, they found shade under another tree. At night, the frail old man was helped to his bed.

Gulipi told stories of the land of the dreamtime, the ancient people and the rainbow serpent. Stories of hunting, fishing and gathering. Stories of the emu, the kangaroo and the turtle. The meaning of ceremonies and dances. He spoke in his native tongue, the one Elke had learned from her mother. Sometimes he drew pictures in the dust with a stick held in his long fingers "These are things that must be told. Things that must be learned by your children and their children and all the children after that," he said.

At the end of the second day, Gulipi had finished his speaking. He had told all. He leaned back against the boab tree and closed his eyes, a smile on his weary old face. He had gone to join his ancestors.

Elke gently kissed his forehead. "Thank you, Gulipi," she whispered. The spirit of her ancestors and of the land had joined her own. Tomorrow she would return home.

Father's Photo

As much as I love my brothers, I wish, as I have done countless times, I had a sister. Not that they shirk their duties. Far from it. As soon as they heard the news, they came. Edwin hurried from Broken Hill; Gerald from Albury and Thomas from Brisbane. They were with me at Mother's bedside when she closed her eyes for the last time.

Now they've gone to discuss Mother's will with her Solicitor. I wanted to be involved, of course, but they thought it not necessary. "We men will take care of that," Edwin said. Being the oldest, I guess he feels duty bound to deal with such matters.

"You live closer than we do, Imogen. It will be easier for you to sort out Mother's personal effects." Thomas seems to have forgotten that the journey from Liverpool to Balmain is quite long.

My brothers are united in their belief that it is my role to deal with Mother's personal effects. Though honoured, I am already exhausted. Mother's death has taken a toll on me. At times, I feel If might drown in my tears. At other times, I am incapable of doing anything useful because a heavy black mantle wraps around my soul, saps my energy and utterly destroys my ability to think sensibly. My brothers are stoic and dry eyed, though their suffering surely equals mine. I so long for a tearful embrace and the outpouring of emotion only women can share.

Not knowing where to start, I gathered photos from mantle pieces and side tables. What will we do with them? How can we dispose of things that were precious to Mother?

Are they now worthless? It seems so disrespectful. Once again, tears threaten to drown me. I gaze at a silver framed photo and, suddenly, fifty odd years have been brushed aside like cobwebs. It's a photo of Mother, the boys and myself. Edwin was ten, Gerald nine, Thomas seven. I was only five at the time but still remember the day.

We had lived in this very street, Stephen Street, right near the end where it intersects with George Street. Mother was very proud of that little rented house, always keeping it clean and welcoming. It's gone now, replaced by a grocers shop with living quarters above. We moved from that house when I was ten.

I don't recall the exact day the photo was taken. The boys were pleased about having a day off school so it must have been a week day. The night before, Mother painstakingly twisted my long straight hair around strips of old linen. "You will have the prettiest curls ever." I had never heard Mother tell a lie so I believed her. I was very excited by the thought of those curls, though I had to sleep on my stomach to avoid discomfort.

Father woke us early on the day. There was a feeling of tension in the air. I knew it had something to do with The War. I didn't know what The War was about, only that it worried grownups; that hundreds of men went "overseas" and many came back crippled or missing a limb. Others never returned. I wished The War would go away.

We ate our porridge in tense silence. "Elbows off the table!" Father gave Gerald a playful push. He had always joked a lot. Now it seemed that any playfulness or jolliness from Mother or Father was somehow forced.

"Will you come back, Father?" I couldn't imagine life without him.

"Of course." He poured himself a cup of tea. Mother started clearing the table.

The boys started to quarrel about drying the dishes. "I did it yesterday, it's your turn." Thomas threw a tea towel at Gerald.

"I set the table." Edwin gave Gerald a shove."

"That's no way to behave for someone who will the man of the house when I'm away." Edwin seemed to grow more quarrelsome each time Father spoke in this vein. Mother intensified her scrubbing of the porridge pot.

Father had given us a lot more hugs lately. That morning was no exception. "Be good children," he said as he left for the Central Railway Yards. He took great pride in his work building railway carriages. I thought he was very clever.

Mother admonished us to stay clean as we donned our best clothes. When she removed the rags from our hair, I ran to a mirror and stared in amazement. I had never seen such beautiful curls.

I remember, too, how beautiful Mother looked. She wore her blue dress. Her shiny brown hair was held in place with long bobby pins. She applied a little bit of rouge, powder and lipstick. I wished I could do the same.

We walked to the photographer's shop in George Street where we endured a great deal of bullying by the humourless, moustachioed photographer. It's a miracle we managed to look anything but grumpy in the photo.

"Why does Father want our photo?" I asked Mother on the way home.

"So that he can look at us every day."

"How long will he be gone?" Edwin asked. Perhaps he was worried about being the man of the house.

The answer was far from satisfactory. "As long as it takes."

Father seemed to be gone for an eternity. In reality, it was a year. When he left to go to that mysterious war, he was a splendid looking man, tall and straight with proud brown eyes. He was different when he came back. There was barely enough flesh to cover his bones. He was changed in other ways as well. Half of one leg was missing and his eyes often held a faraway look.

Father never spoke about The War and somehow conveyed to us that we shouldn't enquire. He did speak longingly, however of his former work. Office work left him restless. At times, he became quite irritable. Then he would find someplace where he could be alone. No doubt, all those stifled emotions and unfulfilled dreams contributed to his early demise.

Mother, so serene and beautiful in the photo, rarely complained and remained dignified to the end. Edwin tried to be the man of the house after Father's death but he was just a boy so it was all left to Mother. I wish I could have her back again.

Tears continue to fall as I shift my gaze to the young boys in the photo, they have grown into good men, tough on the outside but kind and gentle on the inside. I live them dearly.

I look at the little girl with the long curls seated in front of the boys. My hair is grey and shorter now. I am satisfied with my life, in spite of difficulties and regretful mistakes. Weariness will not deter me from the task ahead. I will know what to do. Mother's spirit will guide me.

A Gift from God

The ashes were still warm though the fire in the hearth had died. A greasy scum lay on top of the pot of chicken soup. Dirty dishes from last evening's supper were scattered on the table. Ants trailed up a table leg to a half-eaten loaf of bread.

Henrietta sat in a rocking chair near the hearth. Her tear streaked face pale and puffy, her blue eyes staring into space. Milk oozing from her swollen breasts seeped through her undergarments and saturated her bodice. Oozing breasts reminding her of her loss.

After four years of marriage, she hadn't produced a child. She consulted apothecaries and tried many remedies; eventually resigning herself to being barren. She ignored the whispers and gossip. She told her husband, Ludwig that she understood if he wished to find another wife.

Then when snow lay heavily on the earth, Henrietta discovered she was with child. She cried tears of joy. Those who had mocked now brought gifts for the baby and herbs to help with the birth. Ludwig's step seemed lighter and he whistled while he fashioned a wooden crib.

The baby came swiftly and early. Ludwig had taken two geese to the market leaving Henrietta hanging herbs on a drying rack outside the door. A sharp pain in her belly made her gasp. The next one caused her to scream. She staggered inside to her bed as the pains became more frequent and more intense.

Ludwig arrived home to find Henrietta sitting in the rocking chair nursing their daughter. The baby was small, too small, but perfectly formed with her mother's blue eyes and her father's dark hair. "I want to name her Charlotte Rose," Henrietta said. They kissed and caressed her, giving thanks to God.

Three weeks later, Ludwig woke to find Charlotte Rose still and lifeless in her crib. Their grief was immeasurable. The people of the village offered comfort and told Henrietta she would find herself with child again before long. Henrietta stared into space and refused to swallow the broth Ludwig forced between her lips. Ludwig feared that she, too, would die. He went to find the old Medicine Woman.

A faint cry, like that of a hungry baby, wakened Henrietta from her stupor. "Charlotte Rose, don't cry. I have plenty of milk for you." More milk seeped through her bodice.

Staring at the empty crib, she heard another cry. "Where are you, my darling?"

The crying became more persistent, like a thin wail. Frantically, Henrietta ran from room to room searching the cottage. The cry came again and she ran out the door, almost treading on a bundle of rags laying on the step.

Kneeling, she pulled the rags apart. "Charlotte Rose, where have you been?" The baby's face was red with rage. Blue eyes peeped from puckered lids and tiny fists beat the air.

"Shush now little one." Henrietta sat on the step, undid her bodice and nestled the baby to her breast where it drank hungrily. Charlotte Rose seemed to have changed in some inexplicable way but Henrietta didn't dwell on that. Her arms were cradling a warm baby and her breast was giving it sustenance. In a soft, gentle voice, she sang a lullaby she had learned from her own mother.

The baby fell asleep, milk dribbling from a corner of

its mouth. Henrietta remembered a tiny baby girl being lowered into a grave in the church yard. She remembered the tears streaming from Ludwig's eyes. She remembered falling to the ground and begging God to bring back her child.

Perhaps that had all been a bad dream. She looked down at the sleeping baby then slowly examined it. It was longer and thinner than she had remembered Charlotte Rose. Could a baby change so much in just a week? Where had the rags come from? She unwrapped the baby, gazing at its body, its thin legs, and its perfect feet. Then she saw the tiny appendage between its legs. She touched the little grub like thing to make sure she hadn't imagined it then stroked the little empty sac behind it.

This was not Charlotte Rose. This was a boy. God must have sent him to her. She suspected that Ludwig had secretly wanted a boy and God must have known.

Ludwig and the old Medicine Woman found her leaning against the door post, her eyes closed in sleep. The baby was nestled against her breast.

Henrietta's story was hard to believe and she was accused of stealing the baby. The village people cried, "Throw her in prison," but the old Medicine Woman said, "The baby needs milk and no one else can provide that. It wouldn't be right to throw a babe in prison and if we take him from her, he will starve to death."

Scouts were sent to other villages and farm houses and to cottages in the woods. There were no reports of a stolen baby.

Henrietta and the baby both grew strong. Henrietta was so happy and Ludwig couldn't bear the thought of the baby being taken from her. She named the baby Manna because he was a gift from heaven sent from God. The priest refused to baptise him.

Ludwig had seen the red mark on the sole of Manna's left foot. It was roughly the shape of a witch hat. His heart filled with fear for surely the birth mark was a sign that the baby was the son of a witch. Henrietta said, "It is nothing but a tiny mark." Just the same, they kept his feet covered with booties so that others would not see the mark.

Three years later, on a bitterly cold winter night, as Henrietta and Ludwig were preparing for bed, there was a loud rap on the door. Cautioning Henrietta not to follow, Ludwig took a poker from the hearth and opened the door. An old man stood on the step. His woollen cap and great coat were covered in snow. His lined, whiskery face was reddened from the cold. He carried a hessian bag in one hand.

"What do you want?" Ludwig asked.

"I am sorry to bother you so late at night. I've travelled from a place far to the North hoping to find a relative. I fear I may be lost and hope you might give me shelter for the night."

The man looked so wretched; they invited him in to warm himself by the fire. When he had eaten some hot soup and some bread, they gave him a blanket and said he could sleep by the hearth. He said his name was Willem and he would not harm them.

The next morning, Ludwig found the old man setting a pot of water on the newly lit fire. Manna toddled into the room and stared at the stranger. Henrietta quickly put shoes on the child's bare feet.

Henrietta served steaming bowls of porridge and wondered when the stranger might leave. "Where does your relative live?"

"The last I heard, he was around these parts." The old

man bent his head and busied himself eating porridge.

The little boy watched intently. As the old man ate the last spoon full, Manna clapped his hands and said, "Good boy! All gone."

Willem's eyes filled with tears. "I have a story to tell. A confession to make."

They looked at him expectantly. "Go on," urged Ludwig.

"I was married to a beautiful woman who was many years younger than me. A little over three years ago, she gave birth to a baby boy. He was perfect in every way, except for a mark shaped like a witch hat on the sole of his left foot."

Henrietta gasped and gathered Manna to her bosom. Ludwig rose and stood in front of her.

The old man continued, "The midwife said the mark meant the baby was the son of a witch. She ran off to fetch the priest. I didn't dare tell her I have the same mark on my left foot.

Soon our cottage was surrounded by people shouting for my wife and son to be burnt at the stake. My wife was too weak to flee but she begged me to go taking the baby with me. 'They will kill us both. It is best that you at least save our son.'

"I climbed out a back window and fled with our son. I travelled for days, barely stopping to rest. I stole milk from cows and goats but the baby didn't like the taste so he became weak and thin. When I reached your cottage, I peered through a window and saw a woman sitting motionless in the rocking chair while breast milk stained her clothes. I left my son on your door step, praying you would care for him."

Henrietta shouted, "He is our child and you have no right to him."

"Yes, my dear, he is your child now. All I ask is that I may visit him."

Henrietta and Ludwig felt indebted to the old man for, without him, they would not have Manna. So Willem stayed on, often bouncing Manna on his knee and telling tales of far off places.

Two years after his arrival, when ill health was beginning to bend and weaken him, Willem said it was time to leave. All their tears and protests were in vain. He accepted some food and two blankets and set off down the road towards the North.

They heard that the old man had died whilst kneeling in the village square where his wife had been burned at stake. He was buried, fully clothed, in a far corner of the graveyard, far from the other graves. It was spring time and the birds were singing when Henrietta placed a wreath of wild flowers on his grave and whispered a tearful prayer.

The Short and Twisted Man

Short and twisted
That's what he was.
No one knew if he was always that way
In fact, no one knew his age.
It seemed like he'd been around
Forever. Sitting there chewing a match stick
Forever.
His short and twisted body
Resting on an old couch
With busted leather
And stuffing and springs
Poking out.
Short and twisted springs.

Every day he walked to the shop
On his short and twisted legs
With trousers rolled up.
His trousers were too long
But he rolled them too high
And his legs
White and short and twisted

Were on show
Between his trousers and his socks.
He walked to the shop for a paper
Then walked home
On his short and twisted legs
And sat on the couch
With its short and twisted springs poking out.
He read the paper from end to end
All the while chewing on a match stick.

He's not there anymore
The short and twisted man,
Not sitting on the couch
With the short and twisted springs poking out
Reading the newspaper
Chewing on a match stick.
They put his body
His short and twisted body
In a pine box
A box all smooth and straight.
A priest with a bald head
Said a prayer
A short little prayer
And they put him in the ground.

I'm sitting on his porch
Resting on his couch
With busted leather
And stuffing and springs poking out
Short and twisted springs,
I'm reading the newspaper
Chewing on a match stick.
I'm thinking about life
Thinking how short and twisted
Life can be.

The River

A hot wind rustled the dry leaves of eucalyptus trees and raised dust where there had once been green grass and shrubs. The sun burned through her light clothing as she walked along the banks of the river. Before the long drought, the river had been wide and deep. Now it was a series of muddy waterholes. The smell of rotting fish trapped in the mud filled and assaulted Hannah's nostrils.

Her mind was filled with thoughts of her marriage. She had married Geoffrey following a whirlwind romance. He was steady and reliable, a solid rock to balance her impetuous nature. Everyone said, "He will keep you anchored while you write books and create wonderful pottery." Before long, good solid Geoffrey wanted her to be just like him, dull and unimaginative. "I will suffocate," she thought. "Just like the fish in those putrid waterholes."

She returned to the studio, where the clay in her hands turned to dead fish, her pen wrote about suffocation. Geoffrey said, "You aren't earning much from pottery or writing. There's a vacancy in my office for an administrative assistant." She was duly appointed. At night she dreamed about drowning in grey mud that stank of dead fish.

The long drought broke and swamps formed where there once was dust. The putrid waterholes filled and swelled. The river returned to its former grandeur. Geoffrey planted a new lawn in front of their house.

Hannah was promoted to a higher post and given a framed award certificate for being voted the best administrative officer of the year. She was an expert at answering phone calls and using computerised filing systems. The clay in her studio dried and crumbled. Her hands became clumsy; her mind was filled with spreadsheets.

The river, full and vibrant, wound through the land towards the ocean. Beneath its water, there was an abundance of life; fish crayfish, turtles and a myriad of other creatures. Ducks and pelicans scooted across its surface or waded in its shallows. Other birds nested in the trees along the banks. Hannah quit her job, left Geoffrey and moved to a place of her own.

She parked her car on a high cliff and walked to the edge. Far below, the river met the ocean in a frothy churning whirlpool. From her bag she took her framed award certificate and a bundle of photos of Geoffrey. She dropped them over the edge and watched as they were sucked into the swirling water.

The next day, the clay in her hands turned into frolicking dolphins. In her mind, she wrote stories about songbirds, laughter and skipping just for the joy of it.

No Breeze to Carry the Sound

He would come looking for her. He always did. If she didn't return of her own accord, she would suffer more pain, more humiliation. She promised herself that one day she would leave for good; go somewhere he wouldn't find her. Right now, her face bruised and bleeding, her dress torn and wet and her feet bare, she had no choice but to trudge back to the man she hated.

Henrietta crawled out from beneath the upturned wooden boat where she had sheltered while a wild storm lashed the coast during the night. She sat, leaning against the rough timber with its peeling blue paint and licked her cut lip. Then, gingerly, she examined her face with her fingertips. She probably needed stitches above her left eye but she would pull the split edges together with sticking plaster.

If she went to a doctor, she would be called "dear" and advised to see a social worker. She knew more than any social worker. She knew Apprehended Violence Orders didn't work. She knew that safe houses weren't safe.

She heard the squawking of sea gulls and the gentle lapping of water. Otherwise, the beach was quiet and peaceful. Pink smudges from the rising sun streaked the sky. Tiny crabs scuttling sideways across the sand, seemingly unaware of Henrietta's presence.

She decided to rest a while longer. The solitude and cool sea air might help her gather some strength before she returned to the monster. She must take the long route along the shoreline. There was a shorter route up over the cliff but she had no energy to attempt that.

She leant against the boat and closed her eyes, postponing the moment when she would have to face Jake. He would be waiting. Sitting on the step. "Knew you'd come crawling back," he'd say. "I'm not waiting all day for my breakfast," he'd say.

Jake had been kind, charming, romantic, handsome and the perfect gentleman. Henrietta had been drawn to him, fascinated and blinded by love. He was still handsome but she had soon learned that he possessed a cruel streak so ugly it was beyond comprehension.

Slowly, she rose to her feet and stood still while a wave of dizziness passed. She should leave while it was still early, before people were out and about. She didn't want to be seen in this state. She took a few steps, feeling the soft sand beneath her feet.

She glanced towards the cliff and froze. Silhouetted against the sun, a figure stood at the edge of the cliff amongst the stunted trees and shrubs. At any moment, he would scramble down the cliff over the rocks and onto the beach. She had no strength to out run him. She stood watching and waiting for her punishment.

The figure moved closer to the edge. There was no breeze to carry the sound but she heard anyway. "I will teach you a lesson you will never forget!"

Then Henrietta heard a tiny rumble, a whoosh and a sound like the rattling of pebbles. She watched as the edge of the cliff broke away, crumbling as it hurtled to the beach below. She saw him there. Saw him tumbling with the soil and rocks and uprooted trees, shrubs and grass. Saw his limbs flailing in the air, as though he might find a toe hold or something to grip. Then he disappeared amid the rubble.

She stared at the cliff, torn and ragged as if giant blunt scissors had hacked part of it away. The roots of trees and shrubs hung like loose threads. There was no breeze to carry the sound. No one else would have heard the screams. Henrietta turned towards the path along the beach.

Tomorrow

Squatting down, the woman dangled a piece of chicken meat from her outstretched hand. A dog watched her from behind the trunk of an apricot tree which provided no protection whatsoever and offered no concealment but was a barrier between animal and human; something to hinder the woman from moving closer.

The dog stood motionless, gingery brown coat shining in the warm sunlight, tension in its long body and short legs. Watching for danger, its amber eyes flicked over the woman, the outstretched hand and the chicken meat. Its nostrils flared almost imperceptibly but its head didn't move. A thread of saliva escaped from its closed mouth.

"Come on Flossie," the woman said in a coaxing voice. "Come on girl. This is for you."

With no indication of recognition or pleasure in its eyes, the dog darted forward, snatched the chicken meat and ran back behind the apricot tree. She swallowed the meat without chewing it.

Sighing, the woman stood and straightened her back. She knew all along that the dog would snatch the chicken meat. A few minutes earlier, Flossie had gobbled down a bowl of food, all the while watching in case it was whisked away from her. Afterwards, as was her habit, the woman offered the chicken meat as a treat. The woman wanted Flossie to know she had a friend. The dog always feigned disinterest at first, but would eventually succumb to the temptation. She always came back for second helpings.

The woman remembered Flossie arriving at Paradise

Animal Sanctuary four years ago. A breeder had advertised her as "Free to a good home." The family who took her had been loving and caring for but these were foreign concepts for Flossie. Before long, she arrived at the sanctuary.

The sanctuary staff suspected the dog had lived in a cage and had been used as a breeding machine, producing one litter of pups after the other. She had probably eventually produced a litter of pups that had died or had been too malformed to be sold. Flossie was of no further use to the breeder so she was discarded like a piece of rubbish

At just three years of age, Flossie's reproductive system had been worn out. She had arrived at the sanctuary emaciated and with a matted coat but her odd shaped body was still basically strong. It was the unseen things that were the most damaged. Her mind was broken, her spirit extinguished, her soul shrivelled and sunken into itself.

The woman knew there was no point in trying to touch the dog. In spite of her awkward looking body, Flossie's movements were swift. Her amber eyes devoid of emotion, Flossie would watch every move the woman made then, at the first opportunity, scuttle past like a cunning rat.

Just last week, the woman had crept up on Flossie while she was sleeping. Kneeling beside the dog, she gently stoked her back, running her fingers through the silky coat. The dog opened her eyes but didn't acknowledge the woman's presence or her touch. The woman stroked the soft ears and the rubbery black nose murmuring, "Good girl, Beautiful girl." Flossie stared straight ahead, unblinking and motionless. It was always like that.

During the many years she had worked in the sanctuary, the woman had seen things she would have preferred not to. She had witnessed the result of unimaginable cruelty and neglect the human race inflicted on creatures considered to be inferior. No matter how they had suffered, the animals would eventually respond to care and attention, some taking longer than others. They mended, body and soul, even though a few scars remained. Flossie was different. Her spirit was too broken to be mended.

Deep inside the woman there was a terrible ache that couldn't be soothed. She wanted to bathe the dog in the essence of love but she would first have to tear away the hard shell Flossie had built around herself. The woman began to understand the pain that builds such a shell.

There had been a meeting of the sanctuary manager, the staff, a dog whisperer and others. It was a long meeting with lots of discussion and some disagreements. Eventually, a decision was made. The sanctuary was proud of a reputation for never failing and today's decision was not seen to spoil that reputation. It was seen as an act of kindness.

After four years of loving care, the gingery brown dog known as Flossie remained unhappy and unsocial. It was cruel and unethical to leave a dog in such misery. Tomorrow, the Vet would come and Flossie's misery would end.

The woman wiped tears from her eyes. Tomorrow, Flossie would not come for second helpings.

Ninety Drury Lane

I sensed them creeping through the darkness of night. Lying with my back towards the door, I expected to feel a knife between my shoulder blades at any moment.

My heart beat a frantic tattoo in my chest. I suppressed a primitive scream trying to escape my lips. Maybe they would take my watch and rings, my handbag and laptop then leave.

Something disturbed the air above me and I hoped I was dreaming. My heart beat a deafening tattoo in my ears yet I heard breathing. Not the shallow flutter of my own lungs but the breathing of a stranger.

The darkness above me solidified and stunk of sweat. A whimper, pathetic and dog like, escaped my throat.

A large gloved hand covered my mouth and nose. Other hands pinned my arms. "Not a sound! Just do as you're told." It was a female voice at odds with the large hand covering my face.

The light was turned on and a male ordered me out of bed. Blinking and sucking in air as the hand left my face. I stood with rubbery legs, and looked at four black clad figures, their eyes glittering through slits in black balaclavas. Then I saw the guns. Four of them pointed at me.

"What do you want?" My voice was a whisper.

A gloved hand struck my face, knocking me to the bed. "We ask the questions. You answer them." The female was smaller than the others. I wanted to run but abandoned the thought before it was properly formed. I was surrounded.

"Rosa, where's the tank?" Her eyes were green.

They knew my name. "What tank?" The slap was harder than the first. Blood gave my fear a metallic flavour.

The question was repeated. "I don't know." It was the truth.

"Liar. Where's the tank?"

It made no sense. "I don't know what you mean."

The woman nodded at one of the men who propelled me into the kitchen then tied me to a chair. I didn't struggle. Fear gripped me tighter than the nylon rope cutting into my legs and wrists.

One pointed a gun at my head while the others ransacked my home. I heard them smashing and kicking things. My body trembled. My night shirt was wet with cold sweat, my mouth dry. I told myself to breathe slowly; to count to ten. It didn't work. I became one with fear. It was as if I was watching a horror movie where I was the main character.

I flinched as each piece of crockery shattered on the tiled kitchen floor. The woman bent over me, hissing, "When was the last time you saw the tank?"

"I don't understand what you mean."

"Don't play dumb. We know the tank contacted you. Where is he?"

"I don't know who you mean." I had a fair idea. Three days ago, someone phoned me. A male voice said "Be careful." That's all. I recognised the voice.

The biggest one sat down opposite me. "Let's get this over. Frank owes us big time. Tell us where he is and we will leave." He held my sharpest knife close to my face.

"I don't know." Four years ago, my brother, a big man, left for Brazil. Until the other day, I hadn't heard from him. My cheek stung as the knife sliced it.

"Start talking or there is more of that to come." The woman still crouched over me.

They would kill me anyhow and it wouldn't be quick. A wave of anger I couldn't afford swept over me. "Cowardly thugs, hiding behind hoods. Four against one. I've got nothing to tell you so crawl back to the cockroach nest you came from."

Her punch cracked my nose and toppled the chair. Swallowing blood, I watched her booted foot swing back. I waited for the impact. Wood splintered next to my head as the chair smashed into a cupboard. She followed the chair then stopped mid step at the sound of ring tones. One of the men pulled my phone from his pocket.

The woman laughed a sneering kind of cackle. "A message for you sweetheart."

"Bring clothes. Ninety Drury Lane." The big man snorted. "Gothca Frank. You will have to do without the clothes."

"What about her?"

"Don't waste a bullet." The door clicked behind them.

They would check Drury Lane but not find the number. When we were kids, we lived in a country town. Frank and I had a secret hiding place in an abandoned shack at the end of an overgrown lane. We called it Ninety Drury Lane. We didn't know about Drury Lane in the city.

They would be back.

A Very Normal Letter

Georgina Drake's handwriting had deteriorated just a little but not enough that those who weren't familiar with it would notice. It was still curved and curled and even. Still written with blue ink, though biros had long replaced fountain pens. She regularly wrote letters, rarely longer than two pages, to a handful of people. Her prose was slightly formal and told of mostly mundane things.

Delia was always pleased when she received such a letter. It meant that all was well with her mother. It meant her mother was still of sound mind, hadn't lost her eyesight and was not afflicted by the trembling hands of Parkinson's disease. It meant Delia didn't need to make the long trip to visit her. Well not just yet. It lessened Delia's guilt about not having visited Georgina for nearly a year.

Georgina was prone to hoard things, making Delia worry about the task of sorting things out, packing up if Georgina had to go into care, or, worse, if Georgina died. Georgina wouldn't hear of disposing of things. "It's too early," she'd say. "Perhaps if I were dying..." It was reassuring for Delia to know that she could postpone packing up her mother's home.

The fourth of March was the kind of day when sunshine warmed hearts and dried washing. The postman came early, perhaps wanting to leave early and play with his kids in a park. Delia heard the squeak of his motorbike wheels. She stopped typing to hurry to the letterbox. One of the nice things about working from home was that she could collect her mail the moment it arrived.

There were three letters. A gas bill, a letter from a charity asking for a donation and an envelope addressed in familiar writing. Delia sat down in front of her computer. She opened the gas bill. "Not due. I used less this time." Then she opened the charity letter and threw it in her waste paper basket. "Mum's letter will be the same as ever. I will open it at lunch time."

She stopped for lunch mid-afternoon. Chewing on a sandwich, she opened the envelope addressed in familiar writing. Folded inside the very normal letter from her mother, Delia found a drawing her brother had sent her all those years ago. She recognised it instantly. A ginger cat with a sign saying "Get well soon" attached to its neck. Her older brother was in America as an exchange student when she broke her leg and was admitted to hospital. To cheer her up, he had sent a picture of the host family cat.

Delia stared at the drawing. Why had her mother sent it? There must be something wrong.

The phone rang a few times before Georgina answered it. Her voice had grown thinner and she was a bit vague. "It's lovely to hear you, dear."

"I'm fine. Real fine for a woman my age."

"What drawing was that, dear?"

"Did I send you that?"

"Oh well, you always say I should get rid of things."

There was an early morning plane. Delia didn't tell her mother she was coming.

Georgina's hair had thinned more than her voice. "Such a surprise! I never expected you." Delia suspected her mother was hiding something.

They assured each other they were fine, just fine and

well. They repeated themselves over mugs of coffee. There was the smallest of tremors in Georgina's hand as she held her mug. "Perhaps your brother will come," she said. "I sent him one of his Boy Scouts certificates." Her face didn't change but her eyes twinkled.

The Child

The woman gathered Valerian and placed it in a basket with other herbs and some wild flowers. She was puzzled about why the plant grew so well here by the road but not in her garden. Looking up, she saw that the sky was smudged with pink. She must hurry home for it would soon be dark and she had not brought a lantern with her.

A bundle of rags lay in the long grass. The woman wondered who had left it there and why. She thought to poke it with her booted foot in case something valuable lay underneath. Then she saw that it was not a bundle of rags but a child. A small girl child wearing a cape so dirty its colour couldn't be determined. Long, jet black hair, matted and entwined with twigs and grass covered her face as she slept.

The woman gently touched a hollow cheek. The child stirred and looked up with eyes as black as jasper.

The child was scared. Her heart beat wildly in her chest but she was too tired to scream or run. The woman leaned closer. Her face was fair and freckled, her hair the colour of russet, the same colour as the child's mother's hair.

"Who are you?" The woman's voice was soft and gentle.

The child's name was Darien but she didn't answer. Her mother had said not to tell anyone anything.

The woman asked the question again. The child didn't answer.

"How did you get here?" "Where are you from?" "Where is your mother?"

211

"Can you hear me?"

"Yes," said the child.

"Are you hurt?"

"No." The child sat up, clutching a hessian sack.

"What's in the sack?" There was a half - eaten apple, its flesh soggy and brown.

"My name is Magda. I suppose you had better come with me." The woman scooped the child up in her arms. She was hardly heavier than the basket of herbs and wild flowers.

Magda's arms were strong and she smelled of herbs. The child's mother's herbs had caused trouble. Her mother's herbs, potions and ointments had restored many folk to good health but there were those who said wicked things about her mother. They had taken her away because they believed she was a witch. The child felt a terrible pain inside her. She knew that her heart was broken.

Magda lived on the edge of a town, much bigger than the village where the child had lived. Magda's cottage was bigger, too. There were several rooms instead of two.

Magda stoked the fire in the hearth and warmed some broth for them both. The child ate hungrily for she had eaten very little in several days.

The child grew tired of the questions. She said she didn't remember anything even though she remembered everything, specially her mother's warnings. She and her mother had been happy living in a little cottage which had once been owned by a tinker who left behind many cooking pots and kettles. They had two goats, some chickens and a garden. Her mother was good at growing vegetables and herbs. Sometimes she collected herbs from the roadside, just like Magda.

Magda asked more questions. "Did you run away from your home?"

"I don't remember." Tears streaked her face. She was afraid she would accidently tell.

Magda stroked the girl's arm. "Well, is there anything I haven't asked you about that you would like to tell me?"

The child shook her head.

"I will call you Little Sister. You can stay here until we sort something out. Maybe your memory will return." Tears had washed some of the dirt from the child's face, revealing her dark olive complexion.

Magda washed the child in a tub of warm water then wrapped her in a rug while her hair was dried and brushed. She would have to share Magda's bed and sleep naked as her clothes were so filthy.

The child dreamt of her mother selling cheese, eggs and herbal potions at the village market. She heard her mother's laugh and her soft voice. She felt her touch and smelt her smell. In her sleep, she hummed the songs her mother had taught her.

Magda sat till late at night making new clothes for the child, using one of her own skirts and a jacket of her husband who had died two years before. She was a seamstress and skilled with a needle. Seeing the new clothes, the child was convinced that Magda was trustworthy. Still she claimed to remember nothing about the past, though she remembered everything.

She remembered how some folk said her mother had caused a baby to be born with a crippled leg. Some folk spat at her when they passed her on the street or in a lane. At the market, there were those who refused to buy her mother's goods and others who refused to sell her anything. She thought of leaving and going north but didn't want to leave the chickens and goats.

Every day, Magda took the child to her work place. Customers brought gifts of beautiful fabrics but none recognised her. She was quick to learn and was soon sewing on buttons and even stitching hems. All the while, she thought of her mother and her heart ached. It would be her sixth birthday soon but she wouldn't be able to celebrate because her mother wasn't there and she must not tell anyone.

She remembered the shouting and the stones that were thrown at her mother when a baby was born so deformed, so grotesque, that none could bear to look at it. The parents had taken it into the woods and left it to die. Her mother was very frightened. She had dressed the child in her sturdiest clothes and filled a sack with food and a flask of water. "You must go north towards the mountains. Stay out of sight. Speak to no one. Always go towards the mountains."

The child cried. "I don't want to leave you."

The mother also cried as she hugged her daughter. "Just do as I say. I will always love you. Go towards the mountains. It is important that you don't tell anyone anything. Say you don't remember until..."

There was loud banging on the door and shouts of, "Come out, Ivanka the witch!"

"Quickly! Hide under the bed. When all is quiet, go towards the mountains."

The child heard her mother being slapped. She heard a man shout, "Where is the child?"

Her mother lied. "I sent her to find a chicken that has strayed from the garden." They said they would return for the child later.

The child lost count of how many days she had walked towards the mountains.

Her cheeks filled out and her limbs grew plump. The pain in her heart never left. One day, she overheard a conversation between Magda and a customer. They thought she slept as she lay on a rug in a corner of the room. Magda said she planned to travel south when the weather was warmer. She wished to visit a sister whom she hadn't heard from for many years. Except for her colouring, the child resembled her sister in many ways and it reminded her of how she still loved her sister even though she had run off with a Romany tinker against everyone's wishes. "I heard she had a child who would be about Little Sister's age. Perhaps they could become friends. My sister knew a lot about herbs, I could learn things from her."

The customer enquired about Magda's sister's name. "Ivanka," she replied.

That evening as they ate supper, the child said, "There is something I would like to tell you."

The Painter

He was a tall man, his head almost brushing the top of the doorway. He wasn't exactly handsome but there was definitely something attractive about his weathered face. The grey in his hair suited him. His smile was kind of friendly and his brown eyes looked trustworthy.

Never the less, Moira was wary. He was a painter; a tradesman. She'd had bad experiences with tradesmen. They were quick to take advantage of a woman on her own. They overcharged for shoddy work and fixed things that weren't broken.

She wasn't able to do the paint job herself and this fellow had been highly recommended by her friends. She would take a chance but she would be checking on him. She might even drop in unexpected during her lunch break.

Then there was Billy, the young apprentice, who moved in a clumsy kind of way. She feared he would break something or even fall through a window. She would make sure there was an agreement about paying for any breakages or damages.

She tried to be formal and business like but he insisted she call him "George." She didn't suggest he call her "Moira" instead of "Mrs Smith."

She showed them through the house, explaining what needed to be done. Two shaggy little black dogs followed her. "You can put the dogs out in the back garden, providing the weather is fine. Otherwise, put them in another room if they are in your way."

George bent down and patted each of the dogs. They

216

wagged their tails and licked his hands. "The dogs approve of him. Maybe he's all right," Moira thought.

"What are their names and how old are they?" he asked.

"This one is Jane who is eight. This one is Ted. He's ancient, half blind and half deaf but happy." She scooped Ted up and cuddled him to her bosom. He was special. She remembered how her friend, who rescued abandoned and neglected animals, had begged her to take him. She was reluctant to take such a dirty, scruffy, malnourished and scared little creature that was also half blind and half deaf. Over the last six months, she had grown to love him even though he couldn't last much longer. She hoped the painter and the clumsy apprentice would be kind to him.

She sneaked home in her lunch time on a couple of occasions. George and Billy would be sitting in the back garden eating sandwiches, Jane at their feet. Old Ted was always on George's lap. Moira decided they were tradesmen of a trustworthy kind. In addition, their work was of a high standard and nothing was broken.

On day, Moira stopped to chat while the two men ate their sandwiches. "Do call me Moira," she said.

She was surprised when George phoned her at work. "I've got some bad news, Moira," he said.

"Oh dear! What has happened?" Perhaps Billy had fallen through a window.

"I'm afraid old Ted has died. We'd just finished lunch and he'd eaten a bit of crust. When I lifted him down off my lap, he took a few steps then dropped dead. We tried to resuscitate him but it was too late."

"Oh dear!" she said again. "I knew he didn't have long. I will miss him and so will Jane but at least it was quick."

"What do you want me to do with him?" he asked.

"Would you take a nice blue towel from the bathroom cupboard and wrap him in it then put him somewhere safe until I come home?"

George said he could do that and if she was thinking of burying Ted he could dig a hole. She said under the lemon tree would be a good spot.

George was still there when she arrived home. He'd told the apprentice not to wait. A blue bundle tied with a red ribbon lay on the sofa in the lounge room. Jane sat nearby.

"I hope you don't mind but I took the ribbon from your sewing room," George looked embarrassed.

She didn't mind at all. She knew that ribbon was meant for something special.

Together, they lowered old Ted into the hole and scattered red camellia petals on top of him. The roses were not yet in bloom.

George's eyes were moist as he smoothed the last shovel full of soil over the grave. Watching, Moira thought "I knew all along the painter was a decent kind of fellow."

She asked him to stay for dinner.

These Have I Loved

Vanishing waistline
Overflowing bra
My body nurturing a miracle.
Minute booties
And vests.
Kittens and roses
Embroidered
On soft bunny rugs,
These have I loved.

Nausea
Vomiting.
A bladder gone mad.
Backache
Puffy feet.
These I have not loved.

A passing flutter
The kiss of a butterfly wing.
Soft pokes and prods
From within
Becoming
Strong kicks and pushes.
A growing miracle
Stretching
Growing limbs.
These have I loved.

Cramping pain
A mere annoyance.
Then strong
Frequent
Insistent
Enslaving
Overpowering.
Exhausting

Allowing no rest.
Tearing my body apart.
These I have not loved.

A lusty cry.
A loud protest
Demanding attention.
Wrinkled face
Tiny clenched fists.
Squirming body
Pink
Slimy
Warm.
You I have loved.